The LAST DAY of a CONDEMNED MAN

The LAST DAY of a CONDEMNED MAN

Victor Hugo

Translated from the French by Arabella Ward

New Foreword by David Dow

DOVER PUBLICATIONS, INC.
Mineola, New York

Copyright

Bibliographical Note

This Dover edition, first published in 2009, is an unabridged republication of the work published by Thomas Crowell and Company, New York, in 1896. A new Foreword by David Dow has been prepared for this edition.

Library of Congress Cataloging-in-Publication Data

Hugo, Victor, 1802–1885.
    [Dernier jour d'un condamné. English]
    The last day of a condemned man / Victor Hugo ; translated from the French by Arabella Ward.
        p. cm.
    Originally published: New York : Thomas Crowell & Co., 1896.
    ISBN-13: 978-0-486-46998-0
    ISBN-10: 0-486-46998-0
    I. Ward, Arabella. II. Title.

PQ2285.D413 2009
843'.7—dc22

                                                          2008053681

Manufactured in the United States by LSC Communications
46998007   2019
www.doverpublications.com

Foreword

We do not know his name or exactly what he did. We know little about his present, less about his past, and nothing of his childhood. We do not know the name of his victim, or even with certainty that there was a victim. A book about the death penalty that does not tell us the details of the death of the victim is a rare (perhaps unprecedented) volume, yet that is the book Victor Hugo has written. We know nothing that Hugo believes to be unessential to our judgment, yet we nevertheless know everything Hugo thinks we need to know to conclude that capital punishment is an abomination.

Hugo was forthright about his intention in writing *The Last Day of a Condemned Man*. He abhorred capital punishment. He said the idea for writing the book came to him at the site of an execution: in the public square, as an execution was taking place, a scene Hugo says he walked upon "casually."[1] Hugo wanted to see the death penalty abolished. He did not live to see that happen, but he played a role in its demise. His instrument was this novella.

To make his radical case, Hugo adopted a radical approach. Visit any abolitionist website in the U.S. or peruse any abolitionist tract and you will learn excruciating details of travesties of justice, for the American approach is to focus on particulars. I do not mean this observation as a criticism. On the contrary, the

---

[1] See the essay "Capital Punishment," in *The Works of Victor Hugo* (one-volume edition) (Roslyn, NY: Black's Reader Service Co., 1928), and available on the web at (http://www.angelfire.com/mn3/mixed_lit/hugo_cp.htm).

American abolitionist strategy is sensible, because it is undoubtedly true that the death penalty favors white skin over skin of color and dramatically favors wealthy defendants over poor ones. It is true that defense lawyers in capital cases are often abysmally bad. It is true that racism pervades the criminal justice system, and inserts itself most insidiously in the death penalty domain. It is true that a significant percentage, perhaps as much as a quarter, of the death row population comprises men with serious mental illness; and a handful, perhaps 3 percent, perhaps a bit more, committed no crime at all. Attention to the particulars is a sound tactic—I have used it often myself—because people who care about equality and fairness may have their support of capital punishment eroded upon learning of the inequality and inequity that characterize our death penalty regime.

In the United States, therefore, in literature as well as political discourse, discussions of the death penalty almost invariably pivot on the facts of the specific crime or the particular criminal. Briefs written by prosecutors to justify imposing a death sentence, and opinions written by judges upholding the punishment, recite in punctilious and gory detail the facts of the brutal murder (and what murder is not?)—facts that typically have nothing whatsoever to do with the legal issue before the courts. Yet our moral sense is quieted, or, if not entirely quieted, at least numbed, by these recitations. We can ignore the brutality of an execution and evade the lawlessness that is attendant to it by averting our eyes and closing our rational minds and focusing all our attention on the horrible facts of the crime.

Occasionally, a death sentence is set aside by judicial review. When that occurs, it is again, ironically perhaps, typically the result of unique facts of the case: the police or prosecutors hid a crucial piece of evidence; or all people of color were stricken by prosecutors from the jury; or the accused wrongdoer is mentally retarded, or otherwise not fully morally culpable. For expedience's sake, perhaps, Hugo, abolitionist that he was, may have supported his latter focus on facts, for the result of this attention is that a human life is spared. But then again, if he were to remain true to his conviction that capital punishment is wrong, he might have deemed these facts irrelevant as well, for even they divert our attention from the crux of the matter, which is, quite simply, whether the death penalty is ever morally sound. Speaking of his book, Hugo said: I have tried "to omit any thing of a special, individual, contingent, relative, or modifiable nature."[2] Morality is found in generalizations, and individual cases are the enemy of generalizations. Hugo aimed for universality, for a broad moral claim, and he hit the target in its bull's eye.

Originally published in French in 1829 under the title *Le dernier jour d'un condamné,* Hugo in this short novel strips away all the exterior, contingent, and variable facts—that is to say, all the facts that differ from one crime to another; from one perpetrator to another; from one victim to another; from one courtroom to another, indeed, from one society to another—and he leaves us with naked psychology, the interior of the human mind, the common core of all humanity. His protagonist is a man sentenced to death in France. We know little else. He has a daughter who believes he is already dead. He will face the guillotine, but, as was customary in France in the nineteenth century—and as remains the practice in China and other nations still today—the condemned does not know precisely when he will be executed until the moment is upon him. He expects his stay in prison to last around six weeks, give or take. (Hugo's protagonist is executed at 4 o'clock. He learns the fateful hour has arrived at 3.) He dies amidst a "horrible crowd . . . , a crowd which longs and waits and laughs."

This scene of a public execution will be unfamiliar to contemporary readers. In the U.S., prison authorities carry out executions in relative secret, often in the middle of the night. Members of the media are present; typically, so are family members of the murderer and his victim. But the procedure takes place behind prison walls, with little fanfare and little public interest. It has not always been this way. The last public execution in America did not occur until 1936, when Rainey Bethea was hanged in front of more than 20,000 onlookers in

---

[2] Ibid.

Owensboro, Kentucky. And of course, lynchings, which some scholars regard as thematically connected to the current regime of capital punishment, were not uncommon as long as two decades later, especially in South, and these horrific scenes likewise unfolded in full view of large and boisterous crowds.

In France, executions never moved indoors, as it were; they took place in public, up until the end. There is a certain logic to having heads roll in the streets. If one objective of inflicting this ultimate sanction is to deter other crimes, it seems preferable for the citizenry to know the punishment exists, and to witness its infliction. North Korea uses public executions to intimidate its citizens to this very day. In parts of the Muslim world, public stonings have a carnival atmosphere. But seeing the state kill makes it more difficult to evade the moral question of whether the state ought to kill, and so at last, in 1981, not quite a century after Hugo's death in 1885, France abolished the death penalty, becoming the last nation in western Europe to do so.

Like Hamida Djandoubi, who became the final victim of the French guillotine when he was beheaded in 1977 in Marseille, the character in Hugo's novel also faces execution by guillotine, a tool conceived by Joseph-Ignace Guillotin in 1789 and used for the first time three years later. Decapitation, which had previously been reserved for executing members of the royalty, became France's sole method of execution, replacing hanging, burning, and other methods, on the theory that a speedy cutting off of the head was less cruel than the alternatives for causing death. This same rationale led U.S. jurisdictions two hundred years later, in the early 1980s, to embrace lethal injection as a method of killing. Conceived of by A. Jay Chapman, a medical examiner in Oklahoma, lethal injection was used for the first time when the State of Texas executed Charlie Brooks in 1982. (Texas has since carried out more than 400 executions by lethal injection, a number which accounts for more than one-third of all executions in the U.S.) Of the thirty-six states that execute criminals, all except Nebraska kill inmates with a three-drug combination that initially puts them to sleep, then paralyzes them, and finally induces cardiac arrest. (Nebraska continued to electrocute inmates until the method was declared cruel and unusual by the Nebraska Supreme Court in 2008.) The history of capital punishment, therefore and paradoxically, reveals the state's very unease with the punishment, for the history of capital punishment has been a steady if quixotic quest to identify a mode of bringing about death that is supposedly more humane than its predecessor—until at last the legislature concludes that the taking of human life is inherently cruel, regardless of the method by which the sanction is carried out. Our system of crime and punishment has progressed, so to speak, from stark brutality, to more nuanced bruality, to the recognition that all intentional homicide is brutal, to abolition.

Hugo's protagonist says that the public "see nothing but the execution, and doubtless think that for the condemned there is nothing anterior or subsequent!" Hugo is no theologian. We therefore cannot learn from him whether there is indeed anything subsequent. His interest is in the anterior (and, of course, the present). Hugo understands that the condemned suffers immensely, but not primarily as a direct consequence of the infliction of the punishment. Rather, Hugo's protagonist suffers exquisitely in anticipation of his fate. He tells us what he fears and what he will miss. Because we do not know the details of what he did, we cannot help but see him as a sentient human being, instead of as a depraved killer. Supporters of capital punishment may be unmoved by Hugo's understanding that the condemned suffers immensely, for the common reaction to stories of hardships endured by those awaiting execution is that they do not suffer enough, that they have it better than their victims, that they, unlike their innocent victims, know their fate. At least we can say of this reaction that it is an honest one, revealing the only basis on which capital punishment can be defended: a visceral and unforgiving antipathy toward anyone who wrongfully takes a human life. But as Hugo shows us here, the condemned prisoner is also a human being who loves others and is loved by them, he is a man who loves life on this earth, and who fears the mob that will come for him. We see in him what it is to be a human being: reason coupled with emotion, rationality coupled with appetite, a simple yet potent desire to live on this earth another day. Whether Hugo persuades supporters of the death penalty to abandon their position is for them to say; what is undeniable is that he shows here irrefragably that the objects of our machinery of death are human beings, not mere beasts.

Proponents cite three justifications for their support of the sanction: that it is cheaper than the alternatives, including life in prison; that it deters other crimes; and that it satisfies society's retributive impulse. As we know from extensive documentation, however, the death penalty actually costs more than the alternatives, and there is no reliable evidence at all that it deters. So we are left with the final justification, which is, truth be told, not so much an argument as an explanation. Defending executions by saying that nothing else will satisfy society's retributive impulse could be used with equal efficacy to justify lynching or torture, and it probably has been. If it were sufficient to justify an action on the sole ground that we feel a strong impulse to pursue that action, our world would indeed be a Hobbesian one, yet Hugo recognizes that, with respect to capital punishment, there is no other justification, or at least none that is not facetious.

When asked on CBS's *Sixty Minutes* whether he had seen the video of Saddam Hussein's hanging, President George W. Bush said he had seen part of it. He did not, he told reporter Scott Pelley, watch Saddam fall through the trap door, on the short journey to having his neck broken. Pelley asked him why not. President Bush responded that he is not a "revengeful" person. That might seem like a surprising disclosure from a man who, as Governor of Texas, presided over 152 executions, but it does serve to highlight that there is no other reason—none besides vengeance, now euphemistically known as retribution—for the state to kill.

And that, in the end, is how Hugo succeeds: by showing us a criminal, a prisoner, a mere man, whom we have no urge or impulse to kill or even harm, for whom we feel not disgust or loathing, but empathy. When he laments that he will see no more sunrises and hear no more singing birds, we know exactly what he means, because these are our regrets, too. Whatever he has done, he is still flesh and blood, a living, breathing, fully realized human being, so that when we kill him, by whatever sterile means we accomplish the deed, we have taken a human life, we have committed a homicide, in contravention of the single norm that every society in the history of human civilization has embraced: Thou shalt not kill.

DAVID R. DOW is the University Distinguished Professor at the University of Houston Law Center, where he specializes in contract law, constitutional law and theory, and death penalty law. He is the Founder and Director of the Texas Innocence Network, as well as the Litigation Director at the Texas Defender Service, an organization devoted to securing competent representation for inmates on Texas' death row. Since the early 1990s, Dow has represented nearly one hundred death row inmates in their state and federal appeals. He is the author of more than one hundred professional articles and essays, and four books, including *Executed on a Technicality* (Beacon 2005).

Preface

The only preface to the first editions of this work, published at first without the author's name, were the following lines:—

"There are two ways of accounting for the writing of this book: First, a bundle of torn, yellow papers was found, on which were written, in order, the last thoughts of a poor wretch; second, there was a man, a dreamer, who was given to studying nature for the sake of art. He was a philosopher perhaps, or a poet, I know not just what; but he took hold of this fancy, or rather he let it take hold of him, and he could rid himself of it only by putting it into a book.

"These are the two theories, and the reader may choose the one which pleases him the better."

At the time of the publication of the book, the author did not think it wise to say too much. He preferred to wait, and see if his views were understood. They were; and today he can unmask the political and social ideas which he wished to make popular in this innocent and clearly stated story. He declares, or rather he acknowledges frankly, that the *Last Day of a Condemned Man* is nothing more than a plea, direct or indirect as one pleases, for the abolishment of capital punishment. His idea was to make posterity see in his book, should they read it, not the special plea of such or such a convict, of such or such a criminal (which is always an easy and transient thing), but the general and permanent plea of all criminals, now and forever; it was the great right of humanity urged and pleaded by every voice before mankind, which is the highest court of appeals; it was the ultimate principle, *abhorrescere a sanguine,* established before the existence of the criminal courts themselves; it was the sombre and fatal question which trembles at the foundation of every capital prosecution, under the triple thickness of pathos with which the bloody rhetoric of the people of the king is covered; it was the question of life and death, I say, naked, unclothed, freed from the sonorous subterfuge of the court-room, cruelly brought into the light, laid where it can and must be seen, and where it really is, in its rightful place, its horrible place, not in the court-room, but on the scaffold, not before the judge, but before the hangman.

This is what he aimed to do; and if posterity should ever grant him the glory of having accomplished it, and he hardly dares hope that it will, he would ask for no other crown.

He says, and he repeats it, that he works in the name of every possible prisoner, innocent or guilty, before every court, before every judge, every jury, and every feeling of justice. This book is dedicated to any and every judge. And that the plea may be as great as the cause, he had (and this is why the story was written as it is) to eliminate from the consideration of the subject the discussion of *remote cause* and *inevitable accident, particular case* and *special exception, precedent, mitigating circumstances, story, anecdote, issue,* and *title;* and limit it, if this is limiting, to pleading the condemned man's cause, whensoever he be condemned and whatsoever be his crime. Happy, if without other instrument than his idea, he has searched sufficiently to make a heart bleed under the *aes triplex* of a judge! Happy, if he has roused sympathy for those who believe themselves in the right! Happy, if by searching deep within the heart of the judge, he has occasionally succeeded in finding a man!

When the book appeared, three years ago, there were some who imagined that it was worth while to question if the idea was the author's. Some thought it was taken from an English book, others from an American. Strange mania, to look for the origin of things in a thousand places, and to make the stream which runs through your street start from the mouths of the Nile! No! It was taken neither from an English nor an American nor a Chinese book. The author found the idea of *The Last Day of a*

Condemned Man not in any book,—he is not in the habit of
going so far for his ideas; but he found it where you all may find
it, where, perhaps, you have found it, (for who in his own mind
has not written or dreamed of *The Last Day of a Condemned
Man?*) on the public Place, on the Place de Grève. It was there
that, passing by one day, he found the dread idea lying in a pool
of blood, beneath the crimson arms of the guillotine.

Ever after, each time that at the will of the fatal Thursdays, in
the Court of Appeals, one of the days arrived when the cry of a
death-sentence was heard in Paris; every time that the author
heard beneath his windows those hoarse criers calling the spectators to La Grève,—every time, the dread thought came back
to him, took possession of him, filled his mind with gendarmes
and hangmen, and crowds of spectators; explained to him hour
after hour the last agonies of the wretched sufferer, while he
confesses, while his hair is cut off, while his hands are bound;
called upon him, the poor poet, to tell it all to the world, which
goes on unmindful, attending to its own affairs, while this frightful thing is taking place; urged him, begged him, shook him,
snatched away from him his humorous verses if he happened to
be writing, and killed them before they were half begun;
stopped all his work, intercepted itself between him and all else,
surrounded and beset him on all sides. It was a torture,—a torture which began with the dawn, and which lasted, like that of
the wretch who was being murdered at that very moment, until
four o'clock. Only then, when the *ponens caput expiravit,*
announced by the fatal voice of the clock, was the author able to
breathe again, and find some peace of mind. Finally, one day,—
it was, he thinks, the one after the execution of Ulbach,—he
began to write this book. From that moment he found comfort.
When one of those public crimes, called *legal executions,* was
committed, his conscience told him that he was not conjointly
liable; and he no longer felt that drop of blood on his forehead
which spurted from La Grève upon the head of every member
of the social community.

But this was not enough. To wash one's hands is good, but to
stop the flow of the blood is better.

He knows no higher, no holier, no nobler aim than this,—to

strive for the abolishment of capital punishment. And it is from his heart that he adheres to the wishes and the efforts of the generous men of every nation, who for several years have worked to overthrow the gallows, the only tree which is not uprooted by the Revolution. It is with joy that it comes his turn, his, the poor poet, to apply his axe, and enlarge as much as possible the gash made by Beccaria, sixty years ago, on the old gallows which has stood for so many centuries over Christendom.

We have said that the scaffold is the only thing which Revolutionists do not demolish. It is seldom indeed that a revolution spares human life; and coming, as it does, to prune, cut, hack, and behead society, capital punishment is one of the instruments which it is most loath to give up.

We will admit, however, that if ever a revolution seemed to us worthy and capable of abolishing capital punishment, it was the Revolution of July. It seems to belong to the kindest popular movement of modern times to blot out the barbarous punishment of Louis XI, Richelieu, and Robespierre, and to inscribe on the face of the law the sacredness of human life. 1830 deserved to break the chopper of '93.

We hoped so for an instant. In August, 1830, there was so much generosity, such a spirit of gentleness and progress among the people, and their hearts were looking forward to such a bright future, that it seemed as if, from the very first, capital punishment were abolished from a sense of justice, and by a tacit and general consent, like the other evils which had annoyed us. The people had just made a bonfire of the rubbish of the ancient *régime*. These were the bloody rags. We thought they had been burned in the pile, like the others. And for several weeks, confident and credulous, we trusted in the future, and in the sacredness of life as in the sacredness of liberty.

Scarcely had two months elapsed before an attempt was made to dissolve the sublime legal Utopia of César Bonesana.

Unfortunately the attempt was awkward, clumsy, almost hypocritical, and was made in other interests than the general one.

In October of the year 1830, we remember, that a few days after the Chamber had set aside, by order of the day, the proposition to bury Napoleon under the column, every member began to cry and scream. The question of capital punishment was again brought on the *tapis*, on which occasion we were going to say something, when it seemed that every fibre of every lawyer was seized with a sudden and wonderful pity for any one who spoke or groaned, or raised his hands to heaven. Capital punishment, great God! what a horrible thing! One old attorney-general grew pale in his scarlet robe, he who all his life had eaten bread that had been soaked in the blood of the requisitors, and all at once raised a piteous cry, and called the gods to witness that he was indignant at the guillotine. For two days the court-house was filled with crying haranguers. It was a lamentation, a myriology, a concert of lugubrious psalms, a *"Super flumina Babylonis,"* a *Stabat Mater Dolorosa,* a great symphony in C, with choruses sung by the entire orchestra of orators who occupied the front row of benches in the chamber, and made such beautiful speeches on great occasions. One came with his bass, another with his falsetto. Nothing was wanting. The affair could not have been more pitiful or pathetic. The night session, in particular, was as tender, paternal, and heartrending as the fifth act of Lachaussée. The kind public, which understood nothing of it, had tears in its eyes.[1]

What, then, was the question? The abolishment of capital punishment?

Yes and no.

These are the facts.

Four society men, men of good social standing, such as one meets in a drawing-room, and with whom perhaps one exchanges civilities,—four of these men, I say, had attempted, in the high political circles, one of those bold deeds which Bacon calls *crimes*, and which Machiavelli calls *enterprises*. But whichever they are, the law, cruel to all, punishes them with death. And the four gentlemen were taken prisoners, captives of the law, and

[1] We do not pretend to look with the same scorn upon *all* that was said at this time in the Chamber. Now and then, kind and generous words were spoken. We, like every one else, applauded the dignified and simple speech of Monsieur de Lafayette, and at another time the remarkable words of Monsieur Villemain.

were guarded by three hundred tricolored cockades beneath
the beautiful *ogives* of Vincennes. What was to be done, and
how go about it? You can readily see that it was impossible to
send to La Grève, in a wagon, ignobly bound with great ropes,
and sitting back to back with the officer whose title we must
even refrain from mentioning, four men like you or me, four
society men. If there were a mahogany guillotine—!

Well! There was nothing to do but to abolish capital punishment!

Thereupon the Chamber set to work to do it.

Note, gentlemen, that even yesterday you discussed abolishing this theoretical, imaginary, foolish, poetical Utopia.
Remember that this is not the first time we have tried to call
your attention to the prison-wagon, and the thick ropes, and the
horrible scarlet machine, and that it is strange that this hideous
apparatus all at once springs before your eyes.

Bah! This is indeed the question! It is not on your account,
People, that we abolish capital punishment, but on our own
account, as deputies, and men who may in time be ministers.
We do not want the dreadful guillotine to kill our higher classes.
We overthrow it. So much the better, if that accommodates
every one; but we have thought only of ourselves. Ucalégon
burns. We extinguish the fire. Quick, suppress the hangmen,
blot out the law.

Thus it is that an alloy of egoism alters and changes the most
beautiful social combinations. It is the black vein in the white
marble; it runs everywhere, and suddenly appears every moment
beneath the chisel. Your statue must be done over.

Surely it is not necessary for us to state here, that we are not
of those who demanded the heads of the four ministers. As soon
as these unfortunate men were imprisoned, our indignant anger,
roused by their criminal attempts, changed, as did that of the
world at large, into a profound pity. We remembered the education of some of them, the slightly developed brain of their
leader, a fanatical and obstinate relapser of the conspiracies of
1804, grown gray before his time under the damp shade of the
state-prisons; we remembered the fatal necessity of their common position, the impossibility of stopping on that rapid slide

upon which the monarchy had thrown itself headlong, the 8th of August, 1829, the influence of the royal person, which we did not, until then, sufficiently realize, and especially the dignity spread by one of them, like a purple cloak, over their misfortune. We are of those who wished most sincerely that their lives might be spared, and who were ready to devote themselves toward this end. If ever, by any impossibility, it should happen that their scaffold was erected some day on the Place de Grève, we will not doubt,—and if it is an illusion, we wish to keep it,— we will not doubt but that there would be a riot to overthrow it, and that he who writes these lines would be in this righteous riot. For, it must be admitted also, that at a time of social crises, of all the scaffolds, the political one is the most abominable, the most wicked, the most harmful, the most necessary to have abolished. This kind of guillotine takes root in the pavement, and in a short time pushes forth its shoots at every point.

At the time of a revolution, look out for the first head that falls. It whets the people's appetite.

We were then personally in accord with those who wanted to save the four ministers, and for every reason, sentimental as well as political. Only we would have preferred the Chamber to choose another time for proposing the abolishment of capital punishment.

If this longed-for abolishment had been suggested, not on account of the four ministers who had fallen from the Tuileries to Vincennes, but on account of one of the poor fellows whom you hardly notice when they pass you in the street, to whom you do not speak, whose dusty elbow you instinctively avoid,—the poor fellows who in childhood ran ragged and barefooted in the mud of the streets, shivering on the wharves in winter, warming themselves at the vent-holes of the kitchen of Monsieur Véfour with whom you dine, routing out here and there a crust of bread from the ash-heaps, which they have to wipe off before eating, scraping the stream all day long with a nail to find a liard, and with only the free show of the King's *fête* and the executions at La Grève, the only other free show, for amusement; poor devils, whom hunger drives to theft, and theft to what comes after; children disinherited by a harsh society,

whom the house of correction takes at the age of twelve, the
galleys at eighteen, and the scaffold at forty; poor wretches
whom you could make good, moral, and useful by means of a
school and a workshop, but whom you do not know what to do
with, as you turn them over like a useless bundle, now on the
red ant-hill of Toulon, now in the still enclosure of Clamart,
cutting off life after having taken away their liberty—if it were
in regard to one of these men that you had proposed to abolish
capital punishment, oh, then your session would indeed have
been good and great, holy, majestic, and to be venerated. Since
the august fathers of Thirty, who invited the heretics to their
council in the name of God's entrails, *per viscera Dei*, because
they hoped for their conversion, *quaniam sancta synodus sperat
hæreticorum conversionem*, never did an assembly of men present to the world a more sublime, more illustrious, and more
pitiful spectacle. It has always belonged to the truly great and
strong to care for the weak and feeble. A council of Brahmins
would be beautiful taking up the cause of the *paria;* and in this
case the cause of the *paria* was the cause of the people. By
abolishing capital punishment on this account, and without
waiting until you are interested in the question, you would
accomplish more than a political act, you would do a social
act.

But you have not even accomplished a political act, in trying
to abolish it, not in order to abolish it, but in order to save four
wretched ministers who put their hands upon state policies!

What happened? As you were not sincere, the populace
became defiant. When they saw that you wished to fool them,
they grew angry against the whole question, and, strange fact!
they took sides and argued for that capital punishment, the
whole burden of which they supported. It was your awkward-
ness that brought them to this. By not being perfectly frank, you
compromised the question for a long time. You were playing a
comedy, and they hissed it.

But some wits had the kindness to take this farce seriously.
Immediately after the famous session, the order had been given
to the attorney-generals by a keeper of the seals, an honest man,
to suspend all capital punishment indefinitely. Apparently it was

a great step. Those opposed to capital punishment breathed again. But the illusion did not last long.

The trial of the ministers was brought to a close. Some sentence, I do not know what, was pronounced. The four lives were spared. Ham was chosen as the happy medium between death and liberty. These various arrangements once made, all fear vanished in the minds of the statesmen; and with the fear, humanity disappeared. It was no longer a question of abolishing capital punishment; and once without need of her, Utopia became Utopia again; theory, theory; poetry, poetry.

There always had been in the prisons, however, some unfortunate convicts who, for five or six months, had walked about in the yards, breathing the air, calm, sure of living, taking their respite for their pardon. But wait.

The hangman had had a great fright. The day when he had heard our lawmakers speak of humanity, philanthropy, progress, he thought himself lost; and he hid, the wretch, he cowered down under his guillotine, ill at ease in the July heat, like a night-bird in daylight, trying to make himself forgotten, stopping up his ears, and not daring to breathe. He was not seen for six months. But he had been listening; and he had not heard the Chamber utter his name, nor any of those great expressions of which he was so afraid. No more commentaries on the "Treatise on Crimes and Punishment." They were occupied with entirely different things, of great importance, such as a parochial road, a subsidy for the Opera Comique, or a payment of one hundred thousand francs on an apoplectic budget of fifteen hundred millions. No one thought of him, the hangman. Seeing which, he becomes calm, he puts his head out of his hole, and looks about on every side; he takes one step, then two, like the mouse in La Fontaine; then he ventures out suddenly from under his scaffold; he springs up, mends it, restores it, polishes, caresses it, makes it work and shine, and sets about oiling the old rusty machine that has become out of order through disuse. All at once he turns, seizes by the hair, from the first prison he reaches, one of the poor wretches who have been counting on living, drags him out, strips him, binds him down, and—behold! the executions are begun again!

All this is horrible, but it is history.

Yes, the unhappy captives had a respite of six months; but their punishment was gratuitously aggravated in this way. Then, for no reason or necessity, without knowing why, *for pleasure alone,* the respite was revoked one fine morning, and all these human beings were coldly submitted to a systematic execution. Well, great God! I ask you, what harm would it have done us had they lived? Is there not enough air in France for every one to breathe?

One day a miserable clerk of the chancellor, it matters not who, rose from his chair, saying: "Come! no one thinks any more about the abolishment of capital punishment. It is time to return to the guillotine!" The heart of that man must have been made of stone.

Moreover, never have executions been accompanied by more atrocities than since the revocation of the respite of July. Never has the story of La Grève been more revolting, never has it better proved the wickedness of capital punishment. This increased cruelty is the just punishment of the men who brought back the law of blood with a vengeance. May they be punished by their own deeds! It would only be right.

We must cite here two or three examples of the frightful and impious acts connected with some executions. It would make the wives of the public prosecutors nervous. A woman sometimes has a conscience.

In the South, toward the close of last September (we are not quite sure of the place, day, or the name of the condemned man; but they can all be found if proof is needed, and we think that it was at Pamiers)—toward the close of September, a man was found in prison, quietly playing at cards. He was told that he must die in two hours, which announcement made him tremble in every limb, for he had been forgotten for six months, and had grown to think that he would not have to die. He was shaved, bound, confessed; then they took him in a wheelbarrow between four gendarmes, through the crowd, to the place of execution. Up to this point nothing could have been simpler. It was the usual way of doing such things. When they reached the scaffold, the hangman received him from the priest, led him aside, bound him to the seasaw, *put him into the oven,* so to speak (here I use the slang expression), then let down the chopper. The heavy iron triangle rose with difficulty, fell with jerks into its grooves, and (here the horrors begin) mangled the man, but did not kill him. The victim gave a fearful shriek. The hangman, disconcerted, raised the chopper and let it fall a second time. Again it cut the victim's neck, but did not behead him. He gave a fearful groan, and the crowd groaned too. The hangman once more raised the chopper, hoping the third time for success. Not so. The third blow brought out a third river of blood from the victim's neck, but did not cut off his head. Let us abridge the story. The chopper rose and fell five times; five times it struck the man's neck, five times he shrieked out beneath the blow, raising his head, and crying for mercy! The indignant populace seized some stones, and began throwing them at the hangman. The latter fled under the guillotine, and crouched down behind the horses of the gendarmes. But this is not all. The victim, seeing that he was alone on the scaffold, rose and stood there, a fearful sight, dripping with blood, trying to hold up his half-severed head, which hung down over his shoulder, and imploring them with feeble moans to untie him. The people, filled with pity, were on the point of calling the gendarmes, and coming to the aid of the unhappy wretch who five times had suffered his death-sentence, when a valet of the hangman, a young man of twenty, mounted the scaffold, told the victim to turn over that he might unbind him, and then, taking advantage of the dying man's defenceless position, he jumped on his back, and began with difficulty to hack, with a butcher's knife, at what still remained of his neck. All this happened. All this was seen. It is all true.

According to law, a judge should have been present at the execution. He could have put a stop to it all by a gesture. What was he doing, then, leaning back in his carriage, while a man was being massacred? What was he doing, this punisher of murderers, while in broad daylight, under his very eyes, under his horse's nostrils, under his carriage-window, a man was being murdered?

And the judge was not put on trial! and the hangman was not

put on trial! and no court made inquiries about that monstrous violation of every law on the sacred person of one of God's creatures!

In the seventeenth century, in the barbarous epoch of the criminal law, under Richelieu, under Christopher Fouquet, when Monsieur de Chalais was put to death before le Bouffay of Nantes by a clumsy soldier,—who, instead of a swordthrust, gave him thirty-four blows[2] with a copper's adze,—at least this appeared irregular to the Parliament of Paris: there was an investigation and a trial; and although Richelieu was not punished, although Christopher Fouquet was not punished, the soldier was. An injustice, no doubt, but underneath everything it was right.

In this case, nothing was done. The thing occurred after July, at a time of peace and great progress, a year after the celebrated lamentation of the Chamber on capital punishment. Well! The fact passed absolutely unobserved. The Paris paper published it as an anecdote. No one troubled himself about it. They merely knew that the guillotine had been purposely put out of order by some one who *wished to injure the executor of noble deeds*. It was the hangman's valet, who had been dismissed from service by his employer, and who avenged himself in this way.

It was only a trick. Let us continue.

At Dijon, three months ago, a woman was to be executed, (a woman!). This time also the knife of Doctor Guillotine did poor service. The head was not completely severed; so the hangman's valets took hold of the woman's feet, and in spite of the victim's shrieks, they pulled and tugged, and finally succeeded in jerking the head from the body.

At Paris, we return to the time of the secret executions. As they have not dared to behead on La Grève since July, being cowards and afraid, this is what is done. They recently took from Bicêtre a man who was condemned to die, Desandrieux by name, I think; he was placed in a sort of basket drawn on two wheels, closed on all sides, locked and bolted; then, a gendarme

---

[2] La Porte says twenty-two, but Aubery thirty-four. De Chalais shrieked until the twentieth.

in front and a gendarme at the rear, with little noise and no crowd, the basket was placed on the deserted square of Saint-Jacques. It was then eight o'clock in the morning, scarcely day, but a guillotine had been newly erected for the public, some dozen or more little boys who clustered on the piles of stones about the unlooked-for machine; quickly they dragged the man from the basket, and without giving him time to breathe, stealthily, slyly, shamefully, they cut off his head. That, they call a public and solemn act of justice. Infamous irony!

What do the people of the king understand by the word "civilization"? To what have we come? Justice debased by stratagem and fraud! The law by compromises! Monstrous!

It is, indeed, a fearful thing for society to treat a man condemned to die as though he were a traitor!

But let us be just; the execution was not entirely secret. In the morning, on the cross-ways of Paris, they shouted and sold, as usual, the death-sentence. It seems that there are people who make their living in this way. You understand what I mean, do you not? From an unfortunate man's crime, from his punishment, his agony, his tortures, a commodity is made, a paper which they sell for one sou. Can you imagine anything more hideous than this sou corroded with blood? Who is there who would pick it up?

These are enough facts, and too many. And are they not all horrible?

What have you to say in favor of capital punishment?

We ask the question seriously; and we ask it in order to obtain an answer; we put it to those who are well-versed in criminal law, not to literary haranguers. We know that there are those who take the good of capital punishment as a text for a parody like any other theme. There are others who advocate capital punishment only because they hate such or such an one who opposes it. For them it is a quasiliterary question, a question of persons, of proper names. These are the envious, who are as far from being good lawyers as great artists. Joseph Grippas are no nearer to the Filangieri, than the Torregiani to the Michelangelos, and the Scudérys to the Corneilles.

It is not to them that we speak, but to the men of law, properly so-called, to the logicians, to the reasoners, to those who like capital punishment for its beauty, its goodness, its mercy.

Now let them give their reasons.

Those who judge and condemn say that capital punishment is necessary. In the first place, because they must remove from society one who has already harmed it, and who can harm it again. If this is all, life-imprisonment would suffice. Of what use is death? You say that one can escape from a prison? Make your patrol better. If you do not trust in iron bars, how do you dare to have menageries?

No hangman is needed where the jailer is enough.

But, they say, society must avenge itself; society must punish. Neither the one nor the other. To avenge belongs to the individual; punishment, to God.

Society is between the two. Punishment is above her; vengeance, beneath. She uses nothing so great or so small. She should not "punish to avenge herself;" she should *correct to make better.*" Transform the formula of those versed in criminal law into this, and we would understand it and abide by it.

The third and last reason is left, the theory of example. Examples must be made! We must frighten, by the sight of the fate reserved for criminals, those who are tempted to follow in their footsteps! That is almost word for word the eternal phrase of which every requisitory of the five hundred platforms of France are only more or less sonorous variations. Well! We deny, in the first place, that it is an example. We deny that the sight of punishment produces the desired effect. Far from edifying the people, it demoralizes them, it destroys their every feeling, and therefore their every virtue. There are many proofs, but our argument would be overcrowded if we were to cite them. We will mention merely one fact among a thousand, because it is the latest. It occurred ten days previous to the time we are writing. It was March 5th, the last day of the carnival. At Saint-Pol, immediately after the execution of an incendiary named Louis Camus, a group of masked men came and danced around the still reeking scaffold. So, make examples! The Mardi-Gras will laugh in your face!

If, in spite of experience, you still hold to your usual theory of example, then bring back the sixteenth century, be really formidable; bring back the various modes of punishment, bring back Farinacci, bring back the cross-examining juries; bring back the gallows, the wheel, the funeral-pile, the strappado (rack), the cutting-machine, the quartering, the ditch in which people were buried alive, the vat in which they were boiled alive; bring back to every street in Paris, as though it were an open shop among others, the hideous butcher's stall of the hangman, constantly covered with quivering flesh. Bring back Montfaucon, with its sixteen pillars of stone, its rough sessions, its caves of bones, its motes, its hooks, its chains, its carcasses, its tower of plaster dotted with ravens, its branching gallows, and the odor of dead bodies that the north-east wind wafts in large gusts across the entire Faubourg du Temple. Bring back in its permanence and power this gigantic penthouse of the Paris hangman. Yes! Here is an example indeed. Here is capital punishment that is understood. Here is a system of punishment of some importance. There is something horrible in it, and terrible too.

Or, do as is done in England. In England, which is a commercial country, a smuggler is arrested on the coast of Dover; he is arrested *as an example*, and *as an example* he is left hanging to the gallows; but as the bad air spoils the body, the latter is carefully wrapped in linen which is coated with tar, that it may not have to be renewed very often. O land of economy! To tar those who are hanged!

But, nevertheless, this is somewhat logical. It is the most humane way of understanding the theory of example.

But do you really, seriously believe that you make an example when you wretchedly slaughter a poor man in the most deserted spot of the outside boulevards? On the Grève, in broad daylight, it may pass; but on the square at Saint-Jacques! At eight o'clock in the morning! Who is passing there? Who ever goes by there? Who knows that you are killing a man? For whom is it an example? For the trees of the boulevard apparently.

Do you not see that your public executions are done stealthily? Do you not see that you hide yourselves? That you are afraid and ashamed of your deed? That you stammer absurdly over your *discite justitiam moniti*? That at heart you are troubled, abashed, restless, less sure of being right, won over by the general doubt, that you are cutting off heads mechanically, without knowing very well what you are doing? Do you not feel in your innermost heart that you have at least lost the moral and social idea of the mission of blood which your predecessors, the old lawmakers, carried out with a quiet conscience? At night, do you not turn your head over on your pillow oftener than they? Others before you have advocated capital punishment; but they believed they were in the right, that it was just and good. Jouvenel des Ursins thought himself a judge; Élie de Thorrette thought himself a judge; Laubardemont, La Reynie, and Laffemas considered themselves judges; you, in your innermost soul, are not sure that you are not assassins!

You leave the Grève for Saint-Jacques, the crowd for solitude, daylight for twilight. You do not carry on openly what you do. You hide, I tell you!

Every reason for capital punishment, then, is overthrown. Every syllogism of the platform is set at naught, all the shavings of a *requisition* are swept away and reduced to ashes. The slightest touch of logic destroys all poor reasoning.

Let the people of the king no longer come and ask heads from us as jurymen, from us as men, calling on us, in a soft voice, in the name of the society to be protected, the public prosecution to be assured, the examples to be made.

It is all mere rhetoric, bombast, nothing! A prick of a pin on these hyperboles, and you bring down the swelling. Beneath this soft-sounding talk, you find only hardness of heart, cruelty, barbarity, the desire to show one's zeal, the necessity of gaining one's salary. Keep silent, mandarins! Beneath the judge's velvet paw are felt the nails of the hangman.

It is hard to think in cold blood of what a criminal public prosecutor is. He is a man who makes his living by sending others to the scaffold. He is the official purveyor of places like La Grève. He is a gentleman who has some pretension to style and learning; who is a good speaker, or thinks he is; who can recite a Latin verse when necessary, or two, before carrying out a death-sentence; who strives after effect; who interests his *amour-propre*, O misery! where are involved the lives of others;

who has his own models, his desperate types to copy, his classics, his Bellart, his Marchangy, as one poet has Racine or another Boileau. In an argument, he takes the side of the guillotine; this is his *rôle*, his province. His requisitory is his literary work; he embellishes it with metaphors, he perfumes it with quotations, it must be beautiful for the audience, and pleasing to the ladies. He has his baggage of commonplaces still new for the province, his fine points of elocution, his expressions, his literary style.

He hates the proper word almost as much as do our tragic poets of Delille's school. Do not fear that he will call things by their name, pooh! For any idea of nudity to which you may object he has a complete disguise of epithets and adjectives. He makes Monsieur Sanson presentable. He glosses over the chopper. He stumps the seesaw. He twists the red basket into a paraphrase. You no longer know what it is. It is sweet-sounding and decent. Can you picture him at night, in his office, composing at his ease, and to the best of his ability, the harangue which will raise a scaffold in six weeks? Do you see him sweating with blood and perspiration to fit the head of an accused man into the most fatal article of the code of law? Do you see him cutting off a wretch's head with a poorly made law? See how he inserts into a mess of tropes and synecdoches two or three poisonous texts, in order to express and extract at great pains the death of a man. Is it not true that while he writes, he probably has the hangman crouching at his feet, beneath his table, in the dark; and that he stops writing from time to time to say to him, like a master to his dog, "Lie still there! Lie still! You shall have your bone"?

In his private life this public man may be an honest fellow, a good father, a good son, a kind husband and friend, and all the epithets of Père-Lachaise read.

Let us hope that the day is at hand when the law will abolish these mournful duties. The atmosphere of our civilization alone should use capital punishment.

One is sometimes tempted to believe that the advocates of capital punishment have not carefully reflected on what it is. But weigh in the scales of some crime this exorbitant right which society takes upon herself to remove, what she has not

given, this punishment, this most irreparable of irreparable
punishments!

Of two cases this is one:—

The man whom you kill has no family, no relatives, no friends.
In this case he has had no education, no instruction, neither care
for his mind nor for his heart; then, by what right do you kill this
poor orphan? You punish him because in his childhood he crept
on the ground without help and without a protector! You ascribe
to him, as a forfeit, the isolation in which you have left him. You
make a crime of his misfortune! No one taught him to know
what he was doing. The man is ignorant. His fault is in his des-
tiny, not in him. You kill an innocent man. Or, the man has a
family; and then do you think that the blow by which you kill
him hurts him alone? that his father, his mother, his children
will not be disgraced? No. In killing him, you behead his whole
family. And here, again, you kill innocent beings.

Awkward and blind penalty which, turn where it may, kills the
innocent!

Imprison this man, this criminal with a family. In his cell he
can still work for his own. But how can he provide for them in
the depths of the tomb? And can you think without shuddering
of what will become of his little boys, his little girls, whose
father, and consequently their bread, you take away? Are you
counting on this family from which to supply, after fifteen years,
the galleys from the boys, the low music-hall from the girls? Oh,
the poor little innocents!

In the colonies, when a slave receives capital punishment, a
thousand francs indemnity are given to the man's master. What!
you indemnify the master, and not the family! Here, again, do
you not take a man from those who own him? Is he not, by a
more sacred right than that of the slave to the master, the prop-
erty of his father, his wife, his children?

We have already convicted your law of assassination. Now,
here it is convicted of robbery.

Still another point. Do you think of the man's soul? Do you
know its condition? Do you dare to despatch it so freely?
Formerly, at least, the people had some faith; at the final
moment the feeling of religion that was in the air softened the

most hard-hearted; a victim was at the same time a penitent; religion opened one life to him as society closed the other; every soul had a knowledge of God; the scaffold was but the outer gate of heaven. But what hope do you place on the scaffold, now that the mass has no more faith? now that every religion is attacked by the dry-rot, like the old ships which lie unheeded in our ports, and which once discovered, perhaps, worlds? now that little children ridicule God? By what right do you undertake something in which you yourselves doubt the dark souls of your condemned, such souls as Voltaire and Monsieur Pigault-Lebrun have made them? You deliver them into the hands of the priest of the prison, an excellent old man, no doubt; but does he believe, and will he make them believe? Does he not make drudgery of his sublime task? Do you consider him a priest, this good man who jostles against the hangman in the wagon? A writer of soul and talent has said before us: "*It is a horrible thing to keep the hangman, after having sent away the confessor!*"

Those, no doubt, are nothing but "sentimental reasons," some scornful people may say whose logic comes only from their head. To our mind these are the best. We often prefer reasons of sentiment to reasons of judgment. Moreover, the two are always connected; remember that. "*The Treatise on Crimes*" is grafted upon the "*Spirit of the Law.*" Montesquieu engendered Beccaria.

Reason is on our side, feeling is on our side, experience is on our side. In the model states where capital punishment is abolished, the number of capital crimes decreases year after year. Think of this.

However, we do not ask for a sudden and absolute abolishment of capital punishment at once, as was so thoughtlessly advocated by the Chamber of Deputies. On the contrary, we desire every precaution and all possible prudence. Morever, we seek not merely the abolishment of capital punishment, we want a complete change of the punishment in all its forms, from the highest to the lowest, from the lock to the chopper; and time is an element which should enter into such an undertaking, in order that it may be well done. So, on this subject, we hope to develop the system of ideas which we consider practicable. But aside from the partial abolishment in the case of counterfeit money, incendiary, so-called robberies, etc., we ask that from now on, in every capital question, the president put this question to the jury: "Was the accused moved by passion or by interest?" and that in case of the jury's replying, "The accused acted from passion," that he be not condemned to death. This, at least, would spare us some revolting executions. Ulbach and Debacker would be saved. Othello would no longer be guillotined.

Furthermore, that one may not be deceived, this question of capital punishment is developing daily. Before long all society will think as we do.

Let the most obstinate criminal lawyers pay attention to the fact that, for a century, capital punishment has been moderating. It is almost a mild thing now, which shows it is growing weak, and feeble, and approaching death. Torture has disappeared. The wheel has gone. The gallows has gone. Strange fact that the guillotine is a step toward progression.

Monsieur Guillotine was a philanthropist.

Yes, the horrible, voracious Thémis, with her long teeth, the Thémis of Farinace and Vouglaus, Delancre and Isaac Loisel, Oppède and Machauêt, is growing weak. She is wasting away and dying.

La Grève wants her no more. La Grève wants to reinstate herself. The old drinker of blood acted nobly in July. She wants now to lead a better life, and to prove herself worthy of her last beautiful act. She, who for three centuries has been prostituted to every scaffold, is covered with shame. She blushes at her old career. She wishes to forget her evil name. She repels the hangman. She washes her pavement.

Even now capital punishment is carried on outside of Paris. And let us emphasize the fact here, that to go outside of Paris is to go beyond civilization.

The symptoms all appear to be favorable to us. It seems, too, that this hideous machine is disheartened and glum, this monster of wood and iron, which is to Guillotine what Galatea is to Pygmalion. Looked at from one standpoint, the fearful executions which we have described above are good signs. The guillotine hesitates. She fails to strike. The old scaffold for capital punishment is out of order.

The infamous machine will leave France, we are sure; and if God is willing, she will leave it limping, for we shall try and give her some hard blows.

Let her seek hospitality elsewhere, from some barbarous people; not in Turkey, which is growing civilized, nor among the savages, who do not want her (the Parliament of Otahiti has just abolished capital punishment); but let her descend several more rounds of the ladder of civilization; let her go to Spain or to Russia.

The social edifice of the past rests on three columns,—the priest, the king, and the hangman. Long ago a voice cried: "*The gods will it!*" Later a voice shouted: "*The kings will it!*" It is time now for a third voice to cry: "*The hangman wills it!*"

Thus the ancient structure of society will fall, stone after stone; thus Providence will complete the crumbling of the past.

To those who regret the gods, we may therefore say, "God remains." To those who regret the laws, "The country remains." To those who regret the hangman, we have nothing to say.

Nor will order disappear with the hangman; do not think this. The arch of future society will not fall for not having this hideous keystone. Civilization is nothing but a series of successive changes. Which one are you going to help? The change of punishment. The gentle law of Christ will penetrate our laws after a while, and will shine through them. Crime will be looked upon as a malady; and it will have its physicians in place of your judges, its hospitals instead of your prisons. Liberty and health will be one. They will pour balm and oil where the iron and fire have left scars. It will be simple and sublime. The cross will take the place of the gallows. That is all.

March 15, 1832.

THE LAST DAY OF A CONDEMNED MAN

A COMEDY

(Apropos of a Tragedy[1])

---

[1] We think that we should reprint here the following preface in dialogue, which accompanied the fourth edition of *The Last Day of a Condemned Man.* In reading it, one must remember in the midst of what political, moral, and literary troubles the first editions of the book were published (edition of 1832).

Dramatis Personæ

MADAME DE BLINVAL
A CHEVALIER
ERGASTE
A WRITER OF FUNERAL POEMS
A PHILOSOPHER

A STOUT GENTLEMAN
A THIN GENTLEMAN
LADIES
A LACKEY

A Drawing-room

THE WRITER OF FUNERAL POEMS (*reading*).
"Upon the morrow steps were heard within the forest-glade;
A dog barked low beside the stream; and when the little maid
Returned, alas! her bower to find, her heart was filled with
    fear;
For o'er the ancient citadel sad groans assailed her ear;
And never more, oh, gentle maid! oh, gentle maid Isaure!
Shall sing thy minstrel-lover true upon his sweet mandore."
    THE ENTIRE AUDIENCE. Bravo! Charming! Ravishing!
                                             (*Applause.*)
    MADAME DE BLINVAL. There is an indefinable mystery in
the closing words which brings tears to one's eyes.
    THE WRITER OF FUNERAL POEMS (*modestly*). The Climax
is veiled.
    THE CHEVALIER (*shaking his head*). *Mandore, minstrel,*
there is romanticism in that!
    THE WRITER OF FUNERAL POEMS. Yes, sir; but reasonable
and true romanticism. What can you expect? We must make
some concessions.
    THE CHEVALIER. Concessions! concessions! That is how
one loses style. I would give all the romantic stanzas that have
ever been written for this one quatrain:—

        "From Pinde and Cythèra teasing,
           Did Sir Bernard discover,
           That Saturday, the Art of Lover,
           Would sup a' the Art of Pleasing!"

There is true poetry! The art of Loving supping on Saturday with the art of Pleasing! That is fine! But to-day it is the *mandore,* the *minstrel.* We no longer write *fugitive poetry.* If I were a poet, I would write *fugitive poems;* but I am not a poet.

THE WRITER OF FUNERAL POEMS. And yet, funeral poems—

THE CHEVALIER. *Fugitive poems,* sir. (*Aside to* MADAME DE BLINVAL.) Moreover, *châtel* (citadel) is not French; it should be *castel.*

A GUEST (*to* THE WRITER OF FUNERAL POEMS). Allow me to offer a suggestion, sir. You say the *ancient* citadel, why not the *Gothic?*

THE WRITER OF FUNERAL POEMS. *Gothic* is not used in poetry.

THE GUEST. Ah! that is different.

THE WRITER OF FUNERAL POEMS (*continuing*). You know, sir, one must keep within bounds. I am not one who wishes to change French verse, and bring back the epoch of Ronsard and Brébeuf. I am a romanticist, but in moderation. So, with the emotions—I like them gentle, dreamy, melancholy, never bloody and horrible. Let the climax be veiled. I know there are some fools with mad imaginations—By the way, ladies, have you read the latest novel?

THE LADIES. Which one?

THE POET. *The Last Day*—

THE STOUT GENTLEMAN. No more, sir, I beg! I know the book you mean. The title alone makes me nervous.

MADAME DE BLINVAL. It affects me in the same way. It is a frightful book. I have it here.

THE LADIES. Oh! let us see it. (*The book is handed around.*)

A GUEST (*reading*). *The Last Day of a*—

THE STOUT GENTLEMAN. O madame, spare us!

MADAME DE BLINVAL. It really is a dreadful book, it gives one the nightmare and makes one ill.

A LADY (*aside*). I must read it.

THE STOUT GENTLEMAN. We must admit that morality is

growing more depraved every day. Great God, the horrible idea! to develop, study, and analyze, one by one, without an omission, every physical and moral sensation of a man condemned to die. Is it not dreadful? Do you understand, ladies, how any one could write such a thing, or how any one could read it if it were written?

THE CHEVALIER. It is the height of impertinence.

MADAME DE BLINVAL. Who is the author?

THE STOUT GENTLEMAN. There is no name signed to the first edition.

THE POET. It is the same one who has already written other novels, the titles of which I forget just now. The first begins at the Morgue and ends at La Grève. In every chapter there is an ogre who eats a child.

THE STOUT GENTLEMAN. Have you read it, sir?

THE POET. Yes, sir; the scene is laid in Iceland.

THE STOUT GENTLEMAN. In Iceland, how frightful!

THE POET. Besides these, he has written odes, ballads, and I don't know what else, full of monsters who have *corps bleus* (blue bodies).

THE CHEVALIER (*laughing*). *Corbleu!* That would make a tremendous verse.

THE POET. Besides these, he has published a drama—so it is called—in which this fine line is found:—

"*To-morrow, the twenty-fifth of June, one thousand six hundred and fifty-seven.*"

A GUEST. Ah, what a verse!

THE POET. It could be written in figures, you see, ladies:—

"*Tomorrow, June 25, 1657.*"

(*He laughs. They all laugh.*)

THE CHEVALIER. The poetry of the present day is certainly peculiar.

THE STOUT GENTLEMAN. Why, that man does not understand versification. What is his name?

THE POET. His name is as hard to remember as it is to prounce. It has in it something of the Goth, the Visigoth, and the Ostrogoth. (*He laughs*).

MADAME DE BLINVAL. He is a dreadful man.

THE STOUT GENTLEMAN. An abominable man.

A YOUNG LADY. Some one who knows him told me—

THE STOUT GENTLEMAN. Do you know some one who knows him?

A YOUNG LADY. Yes; and he said that the man is very gentle and simple in his habits, that he lives quietly, and spends his days playing with his little children.

A POET. And his nights in dreaming of works infernal.— That is strange; there is a verse which I made unconsciously. But it is a verse, just the same:—

"And his nights in dreaming of works infernal,"

with a good cæsura. There is only the corresponding rhyme to find. I have it! *Sepulchral!*

MADAME DE BLINVAL. *Quidquid tentabat dicere, versus erat.* (Whatever he uttered was a poem.)

THE STOUT GENTLEMAN. You say that the author in question has little children? Impossible, madame, when he has written such a story as this, such a frightful thing!

A GUEST. What object has this novel?

THE POET. I have no idea.

A PHILOSOPHER. It seems to me that it favors the abolishment of capital punishment.

THE STOUT GENTLEMAN. I tell you it is horrible!

THE CHEVALIER. So it is a duel with the hangman?

THE POET. He denounces the guillotine.

THE THIN GENTLEMAN. Yes, I can see that; here are invectives.

THE STOUT GENTLEMAN. Not at all. There are scarcely two pages on capital punishment. It is all sensations.

THE PHILOSOPHER. There he is wrong. The subject deserves discussion. A drama, a novel, proves nothing. Moreover, I have read the book, and it is very bad.

THE POET. It is detestable! Is that art? It is going beyond

bounds; it is speaking out one's mind too freely? Then, this criminal, if we only knew about him! But no. What did he do? We have no idea. Perhaps he was a very bad fellow. One should not rouse interest in one whom we do not know about.

THE STOUT GENTLEMAN. One has no right to make his reader suffer physically. When I see a tragedy, I expect a murder. Well, I am not affected. But this novel makes your hair stand on end and your flesh creep. It gives you bad dreams. I spent two days in bed for having read it.

THE PHILOSOPHER. Besides, the book is cold, premeditated.

THE POET. The book! The book!

THE PHILOSOPHER. Yes. And as you have just remarked, sir, true art does not consist in that sort of thing. I am not interested in an abstraction, a pure entity. I do not find a personality equal to mine. And then the style is neither simple nor clear. It is archaic. That was what you said, was it not?

THE POET. No doubt, no doubt. We must avoid personalities.

THE PHILOSOPHER. The prisoner is not interesting.

THE POET. How could he be? He has committed a crime, and feels no remorse. I would make him just the opposite. This would be the story of my prisoner. Born of honest parents. Good education. Love. Jealousy. A crime, which was not a crime. Then remorse, remorse, much remorse. But human laws are implacable; he must die. Then I would argue the question of capital punishment. There!

MADAME DE BLINVAL. Ah! Ah!

THE PHILOSOPHER. Pardon me. The book, as Monsieur understands it, proves nothing. The particular does not rule the general.

THE POET. Well, better still, why not have taken for the hero, Malesherbes, for instance?—the virtuous Malesherbes? His last day, his punishment? Oh, fine and noble thought! Then I would have cried, I would have shivered, I would have longed to mount the scaffold with him.

THE PHILOSOPHER. Well, *I* should not.

THE CHEVALIER. Nor I. At heart he was a Revolutionist.

THE PHILOSOPHER. The scaffold of Malesherbes would prove nothing against capital punishment in general.

THE STOUT GENTLEMAN. Capital punishment! Of what use is it to discuss that? How does capital punishment concern you? This author must be of low birth, to give us the nightmare from such a subject.

MADAME DE BLINVAL. Ah! yes; he must have an evil heart.

THE STOUT GENTLEMAN. He compels us to look into the prisons, into the galleys, into Bicêtre, all of which is extremely disagreeable. We know, of course, that such places exist; but why should society trouble itself about them?

MADAME DE BLINVAL. The lawmakers were not children.

THE PHILOSOPHER. And yet, if the subject were presented in a true light—

THE THIN GENTLEMAN. That is exactly what is lacking, truth. How can a poet be expected to know about such things? One must at least be a public prosecutor. I read in a newspaper a criticism of this book, in which it said that the prisoner did not utter a word when his death-sentence was read; now, I once saw a prisoner, and when the sentence was read, he gave a great shriek. You see the difference.

THE PHILOSOPHER. Allow—

THE THIN GENTLEMAN. Yes, gentleman, the guillotine, the grave, is poor taste; and to prove this, you see that the book is such as corrupts good taste, and makes you incapable of pure, fresh, naïve emotions. When will the defenders of clean, wholesome literature rise? I should like to be a member of the French Academy, and perhaps my public addresses might make me eligible. Here is Monsieur Ergaste, who is a member. What does he think of the *Last Day of a Condemned Man?*

ERGASTE. Indeed, sir, I have neither read it, nor do I intend to. Yesterday I was dining with Madame de Sénange, and the Marquise de Morival spoke of it to the Duke of Melcourt. They said that there were personalities in it against the magistracy, and especially against President d'Alimont. Abbé Floricour was indignant also. It seems that it contains a chapter against religion, and one against the monarchy. If I were a public prosecutor—

THE CHEVALIER. Yes, indeed, public prosecutor! and the charter! and the liberty of the press! Yet you will acknowledge that it would be disagreeable for a poet who wishes to abolish capital punishment. Ah, ah! under the ancient *régime* any one who published a novel against punishment—! But since the fall of the Bastile one can write anything. Books do a frightful amount of harm.

THE STOUT GENTLEMAN. Frightful. Everything was quiet; we were agitated over nothing. From time to time a head was cut off in France, here and there, two a week at the most, but without noise, without scandal. Nothing was said. No one thought anything of it. And then—this book—a book which gives one a dreadful headache!

THE THIN GENTLEMAN. As though a jury would convict any one after having read it.

ERGASTE. It hurts one's conscience.

MADAME DE BLINVAL. Ah! Books! Books! Who would have thought that of a novel?

THE POET. There is no doubt but that books are poisoning society.

THE THIN GENTLEMAN. Not to mention the language, which these romanticists revolutionize also.

THE POET. Let us make a distinction, sir; there are romanticists and romanticists.

THE THIN GENTLEMAN. Such poor taste, poor taste.

ERGASTE. You are right. It is poor taste.

THE THIN GENTLEMAN. There is nothing more to say.

THE PHILOSOPHER (*leaning over a lady's chair*). Subjects are discussed in this book which are no longer mentioned even in the Rue Mouffetard.

ERGASTE. Ah! the wretched book!

MADAME DE BLINVAL. Oh! do not throw it into the fire. It is hired.

THE CHEVALIER. Talk of *these* times! Since our day everything is depraved. Do you remember our day, Madame de Blinval?

MADAME DE BLINVAL. No, Monsieur, I do not.

THE CHEVALIER. We were the gentlest, the gayest, the wittiest people. There were always beautiful *fêtes* and pretty verses. It was charming. Is there anything more beautiful than Monsieur de La Harpe's madrigal on the great ball given by Madame de Mailly, the marshal's wife, in seventeen hundred and—the year of Damiens' execution.

THE STOUT GENTLEMAN (*sighing*). Those were happy days! Now the morals are horrible as well as the books. Boileu says in his beautiful lines:—

"And the fall of the arts follows the fall of the morals."

THE PHILOSOPHER (*aside to* THE POET). Do they have supper here?

THE POET. Yes, very soon.

THE THIN GENTLEMAN. Now they want to abolish capital punishment; and with this object in view they write novels, cruel, immoral, and in poor taste, like the *Last Day of a Condemned Man* and I don't know what else.

THE STOUT GENTLEMAN. My dear fellow, let us talk no more of this atrocious book; and, by the way, tell me, what are you going to do about that man whose appeal we refused three weeks ago?

THE THIN GENTLEMAN. Oh, be patient a while! I am on a vacation here. Do let me have a breathing space. Wait until I return. If I am away too long, I will write to my substitute—

A SERVANT (*entering*). Madame, supper is served.

Chapter I

Bicêtre

C ONDEMNED TO DIE!
For five weeks this thought has dwelt within me, and this alone, congealing my blood, bearing me down beneath its weight!

Once, and it seems as if it were years and not weeks ago, I was like other men. Each day, each hour, each moment, was full. My mind was young and active, and it delighted in fancies. One after another they unrolled before me, and I saw the rough and scanty stuff of which life is made, with its embroidery of never-ending arabesques. There were young girls, fine copes belonging to bishops, battles won, theatres full of life and light, and then young girls again, and nocturnal promenades beneath the kindly arms of chestnut-trees. My fancy always pictured *fêtes*. I could dream of what pleased me, for I was free then. Now I am a captive. My body is in chains, in a dungeon. My mind is imprisoned in an idea—a horrible, bloody, wild idea! I have but one thought, one conviction, one certainty: I am condemned to die!

Whatever I do, this dread thought is ever with me, like a ghost at my side, alone and jealous, chasing away all other thoughts, face to face with my wretched self, and touching me with its icy hands when I turn away and close my eyes. It glides along every path where my soul would hide, it mingles like a frightful refrain with every word I hear, it clings to the hideous bars of my prison, it pursues me awake, it spies my troubled sleep, and creeps into my dreams under the form of a knife.

I waken with a start, still pursued by it; I cry: "Ah, it is nothing but a dream!"—but scarcely are my heavy eyes half opened, before I see the dread thought written on the horrible reality which surrounds me, on the damp, close floor of my cell, in the pale rays of my night-lamp, in the coarse wool of my garments, on the sombre figure of the sentinel, with his cartridge-box gleaming through the bars. It seems to me that even now, a voice whispers in my ear: Condemned to die!

Chapter II

It was a beautiful morning in August. For three days my trial had been going on; for three days my name and my crime had called together a crowd of spectators, who swooped down upon the benches of the court-room like so many crows around a corpse; for three days the phantasmagoria of judges, witnesses, lawyers, and public prosecutors had been coming and going before me, now grotesque, now bloody, but always dark and dreadful. The first two nights I had not been able to sleep from anxiety and fright; but weariness, physical and mental, brought me rest on the third. At midnight I had left the judges, who were to come to a decision. I was taken back to the straw of my dungeon; and I fell into a deep sleep, a sleep of forgetfulness. That was the first peaceful moment I had had for many a day.

I was still sleeping soundly when they came to waken me. This time the heavy step and the iron shoes of the turnkey, the rattle of his bunch of keys, and the hoarse grinding of the locks, were not enough to rouse me from my lethargy. It needed his rough voice in my ear, and his heavy hand upon my arm. "Get up, will you?" I opened my eyes, and sat up in terror. Just at that instant there fell through the high narrow grating of my cell, upon the ceiling of the adjoining corridor, the only ray of light I had seen for a long time, the yellow reflection, which eyes accustomed to the shade of a prison easily recognize as the sun. I love the sun.

"It is a fair day," I said to the jailer.

For a moment he did not answer, as if doubtful whether it were worth while to waste a word; then with an effort he muttered roughly:—

"Perhaps it is."

I was silent, my mind seemed half asleep, but my lips were smiling, and my eyes were fixed upon the soft ray of gold which illuminated the ceiling.

"It is a beautiful day," I said again.

"Yes," the man returned; "and they are waiting for you."

The words, like a thread which breaks the flight of an insect, brought me violently back to reality. I saw again, like a flash of lightning, the dreary court-room, the horseshoe of the judges which was covered with bloody rags, the three rows of stupid-looking witnesses, the two gendarmes on either side of me, and the swaying black gowns; then, the billowy sea of heads at the farther end of the room, and the fixed gaze of the dozen jurors, who had kept watch while I slept!

I rose; my teeth chattered, my hands trembled, my limbs shook, I could not find my clothes. At my first step I swayed like a man carrying too heavy a burden. But I followed the jailer.

The two gendarmes were waiting at the door of my cell. They put handcuffs on my wrists, and carefully closed the complicated little padlocks. I let them do it; they were machines on a machine.

We crossed an inner court. The brisk morning air revived me. I raised my head. The sky was blue; and the warm rays of the sun, falling across the long chimneys, marked great angles of light on the topmost walls of the dark prison. It was a beautiful day indeed.

We ascended a spiral staircase, crossed a corridor, then another, and still a third, and finally reached a low door that stood open. A heavy odor and the confused murmuring voices came to me; it was the crowd in the court-room. I entered.

At sight of me there rose a clashing of arms and of voices. The benches were hastily moved back, the boards creaked; and as I crossed the room, between two crowds of people, flanked by soldiers, I felt that I was the centre to which were attached the threads which pulled every gaping, staring face.

Suddenly I noticed that I was without irons; but when or where they had been removed I had no idea.

Then a great hush fell upon the room. I was in my place. As the noise and tumult of the crowd ceased, my mind also grew calm; and all at once I saw clearly, what up to then I had realized only in a dazed way, that the decisive moment had come, that I was there to hear my sentence.

Explain it as you will, this thought caused me no terror. The windows were open; the air and the noise of the city fell upon my ears; the room was as bright as if there were to be a wedding there; the sun's rays fell here and there in shining crosses, upon the floor, on the tables, broken by the angles of the wall; and from the shining mouldings of the windows each beam hung in the air, a great prism of shimmering gold.

The judges on the platform had a satisfied air, probably because they had reached a decision. The features of the presiding judge, thrown into soft relief by a ray from one of the windows, looked calm and kind; a young attorney was smoothing out his cravat, and talking gayly to a pretty lady in a red bonnet, who as a mark of special favor had been given a seat behind him.

The jurors alone appeared wearied and discouraged, but I thought they looked so because they had been up all night. Some of them yawned. Nothing in their kindly faces showed that they had just pronounced a death-sentence; they seemed to me as if they wanted nothing but a good night's sleep.

In front of me a window stood wide open. I heard the flower-venders laughing on the quay; and on the window-bench a pretty little yellow plant, bathed in the sunlight, was playing with the wind in a cranny of the wall.

How could a gloomy thought enter into the midst of so many pleasant ones? Surrounded by the outer air and the sunshine, I could think of nothing but liberty; hope glowed within me, like the daylight without; and in perfect confidence I awaited my sentence as one awaits freedom and life.

My lawyer, whom they had been expecting, arrived at last. He had breakfasted heartily. Taking his place, he leaned toward me with a smile.

"I have hope," said he.

"So have I," I replied easily, smiling also.

"Yes," he continued; "although, of course, I know nothing of their decision, still I have no doubt they will refuse to find premeditation, and in that case it will be only penal servitude."

"What do you mean, sir?" I asked indignantly; "I would prefer death, a hundred times! Yes, death!" Besides, some inner voice whispered, what do I risk by saying this? Has a death-sentence ever been pronounced except at twelve o'clock on a cold, drizzling winter night, in a dark and gloomy room, beneath the glare of candles?

It would be impossible in the month of August, at eight o'clock in the morning, on such a beautiful day, and by such a kind jury! And my eyes turned again to the pretty yellow flower playing in the sun.

Then the presiding judge, who had been waiting only for my lawyer, told me to rise. The gendarmes "presented arms;" and as from an electric shock, the entire crowd stood up. A small, insignificant fellow, at a table below the judges, the clerk, I suppose he was, began to read the verdict of the jury. A cold perspiration came from my every limb, and I leaned against the wall to keep from falling.

"Lawyer, have you anything to say as to why the sentence should not be pronounced?" asked the judge.

I had everything to say, but no word came to me. My tongue clove to my mouth.

The defence rose.

I understood that he was trying to soften the decision of the jury, and to substitute for the punishment prescribed, the other suggestion, which had made me so angry.

My indignation must indeed have been great, to make itself felt above the thousand conflicting emotions of my mind. I wanted to shout out what I had already told him: "I prefer death a hundred times!" But breath failed me; and I could only grasp him roughly by the arm, and cry hoarsely, "No!"

The attorney-general began to argue with the lawyer, and I listened with a dazed sort of satisfaction. The judges then with-

drew; after a moment they returned, and the presiding judge
read my sentence.

"Condemned to die!" shouted the crowd; and while they led
me away, the people rushed at my heels with the noise of a falling building. I walked along dazed and stupefied. A change had
taken place in me. Up to the moment of the death-sentence, I
had been living, breathing among other men; now I clearly saw
that there was a high wall between the world and myself.
Nothing seemed the same to me. The great shining windows,
the beautiful sunshine, the clear sky, the pretty flower,—all
were white and dull, like a shroud. The crowd of men, women,
and children following me were like phantoms.

At the foot of the staircase, a dirty black and closely barred
vehicle awaited me. As I stepped in, I happened to glance across
the Square. "A man condemned to die!" cried several passers-
by, running toward the carriage. Through the cloud which
seemed to rise between me and the surrounding objects, I saw
two young girls following me with wide-opened eyes. "Good!"
exclaimed the younger one, clapping her hands, "it will be in six
weeks."

Chapter III

Condemned to die!

Well, why not? *"Men,"* I remember to have read in some book
which contained nothing else that was good, *"Men are all condemned to die with various reprieves."* How is my position any
different?

Since my sentence was pronounced, how many have died
who had expected a long life! How many have gone before me,
who, young, free, and healthy, had counted on seeing my head
fall upon the Place de Grève! How many, even now, may die
before me, who are now living, breathing the glad air, and coming and going as they please!

And then, why should I want to live? The dull light, the black
prison bread, the portion of thin soup, which is brought to me

in a galley's bowl, the harsh treatment I receive from the jailers
and keepers,—I, who am refined and educated,—without a
single human being near me who thinks me worthy of a word or
to whom I can speak, trembling at everything that I have done
and that others are going to do,—these are about the only bless-
ings of which the hangman can rob me.

But, it is horrible!

Chapter IV

The black carriage brought me here, to this hideous Bicêtre.

Seen from afar, the building is somewhat majestic in appearance. It spreads along the horizon, on the brow of a hill, and, in
the distance, still preserves some of its former splendor, the
appearance of a king's château. But as one approaches, the palace is found to be in ruins. The fallen wings hurt one's feelings.
Shame and poverty stare down from the royal façades; it looks
as if there were leprosy behind the walls. It is without windows
or window-frames, with nothing but great iron cross-bars, and
here and there the wan face of a galley or a madman peering
through.

This is a near view of life.

Chapter V

Scarcely had I arrived, before handcuffs were placed on me.
Precautions were redoubled; I was allowed neither knife nor
fork at meals; the *strait-jacket*, a sort of linen bag with wings,
imprisoned my arms. The jailers were responsible for my life. I
had sued for a writ of error; the troublesome business would not
be over for six or seven weeks, and it was important that I should
reach the Place de Grève safe and sound.

During the first few days they treated me with a gentleness
which was horrible. The respect of a jailer savors of the scaffold.

But, happily, after a time, their manner changed. I was handled like the other prisoners, with a common brutality, and received no more of the special and polite attentions which brought the hangman constantly before me. This was not the sole improvement. My youth, my submission, the interest that the prison chaplain took in me, and especially some Latin words which I addressed to the *concierge,* who did not understand them, made them allow me to walk once a week with the other prisoners, without the strait-jacket, which was paralyzing me. After much hesitation, they also allowed me ink, paper, pens, and a night-lamp.

Every Sunday, after service, I am allowed in the yard at the hour of exercise, and then I talk with the prisoners. I have to. They are good fellows, the poor wretches. They tell me of their crimes, which are horrible to hear; but I know that they are boasting. They are teaching me to speak slang, to *"rouscailler bigorne"* (swing the anvil), as they say. It is a language which has grown upon the general language like a hideous excrescence or wart. Sometimes it is strangely forcible and frightfully graphic. For instance: *there is some juice on the trimar* (blood on the road); *to marry the widow* (to be hanged), as if the rope of the hangman were the widow of every one who is hanged. A robber's head has two names, *the Sorbonne,* when it plans, reasons out, and advises crime; the *tronche,* when the hangman cuts it off. Sometimes the language has the wit of a Vaudeville: as *a wicker cashmire* (a rag-picker's basket) *the lyer* (the tongue); and then, everywhere, every instant, strange, mysterious words occur, rough and unseemly, coined, one knows not where, as, *the taule* (the hangman), *the cône* (death), *the placarde* (the place of execution). They use the words *toads* and *spiders.* To hear this language spoken gives one an idea of something dirty and dusty, of a bundle of rags shaken in front of one. But these men pity me, at least, and they are the only ones. The jailers, the wardens, and the turnkeys,—I hate them,—talk and laugh, and discuss me before my very eyes, as if I were a thing.

Chapter VI

I said to myself,—

"Since I have writing materials, why not use them?" But what shall I write? Imprisoned within four stone walls, cold and bare, without space to walk, without a horizon for my eyes, my one diversion consisting in following mechanically throughout the entire day the slow march of the white square which the peep-hole of my door cuts out on the opposite dull wall, and as I just now said, alone with one idea, an idea of crime and punishment, of murder and of death,—is there anything for me to tell, I who have nothing left to do in this world? What would there be in my worn-out and empty brain which would be worth writing?

And yet why not? If everything about me is dull and monotonous, is there not within me a tempest, a strife, a tragedy? Does not this fixed thought which possesses me, appear before me, every hour, every instant, under a new form, more hideous and bloody as the time approaches? Why should I not try to tell myself all that is strange and dreadful in my loneliness. Surely the field is a wide one; and short as my life may be between now and then, there will be plenty of chances to use my pen and ink, in writing of the agony, the terror, and the tortures that assail me. Besides, the only way to lighten my agony is to study it, and writing it will be a distraction to me.

Perhaps, too, what I write will not be wholly useless. This diary of my suffering, hour after hour, minute after minute, torture after torture, if I have strength enough left to carry it up to the moment when it will be *physically* impossible to continue it,—may not this story (necessarily unfinished, but as complete as possible) of my feelings, carry with it a great and mighty lesson? Might there not be more than a lesson for those who convict, in this verbal process of agonizing thought, in this ever-increasing chain of suffering, in this kind of intellectual autopsy of a man condemned to die? Perhaps my story will make them more lenient, when at some future time the question arises of throwing a thinking head, a man's head, into what they call the scales of justice. Perhaps the wretched men have never thought of the slow succession of tortures included under the expeditious form of a death-sentence. Have they ever considered the painful thought that in the man whom they condemn there is an intellect, an intellect which had counted on life, a soul which was not prepared for death? No. In all that, they see only the vertical fall of a triangular knife, thinking, no doubt, that for the condemned man there is nothing before or after.

These leaves will undeceive them. Perhaps they will be published some day, and may make the mind of these men ponder an instant upon mental suffering; for this they do not suspect. They triumph at being able to kill without making the body suffer. Ah! that is what they think! But what is physical suffering when compared to moral? How horrible and pitiful it is that laws should be made thus! The day will come, and perhaps these memoirs, the last confidences of a poor wretch, may help to hasten it. . . .

At least, after my death, may the wind not play in the yard with these sheets of paper, covered with mud; may they not rot in the rain, pasted like stars to the broken window of a jailer's room.

Chapter VII

May all that I write here some day be of use to others; may it keep the judge from pronouncing death sentences; may it save poor wretches, whether they are innocent or not, from the agony to which I am condemned. And yet why? To what end? For what good? When my head is cut off, what difference will it make to me if they cut off other heads? Can I really think of such nonsense as this? Suppose they hurl down the scaffold after I have mounted it! I ask you what good will it do me?

What! the sun, the spring, the flowering fields, the birds who awaken the morning, the clouds, the trees, nature, liberty, life,—have I lost them all?

Ah! It is I who must be saved! Is it really true that this cannot be, that I must die to-morrow, to-day perhaps; is this true? O God! What a horrible idea it is to dash out one's brains against the walls of one's prison!

Chapter VIII

Let me count the time that still remains. Three days' stay after the sentence, for the writ of error.

Eight days of oblivion before the Court of Appeals, after which the *briefs*, as they are called, are filed with the clerk.

Fifteen days delay at the clerk's, who does not know that they even exist, and who, nevertheless, is supposed to have transmitted them, after examination, to the Court of Appeals.

There, each one is classified, numbered, and registered; for the guillotine is crowded, and each must go in turn.

Fifteen days to watch for something which may not favor you in the end. Finally, the Court sits, usually on a Thursday, rejects twenty writs together, sends them all back to the clerk, who in turn sends them to the attorney-general, who transmits them to the hangman. Three days.

On the morning of the fourth, the deputy of the attorney-general says to himself, as he ties his cravat, "We must bring this case to a close." Then, if the deputy clerk is not kept at home by a breakfast with some friends, the warrant of execution is drawn up, written, copied fair, and despatched; and the following day at dawn a frame is heard being erected on the Place de Grève, and in the streets criers are shouting with hoarse voices.

Six weeks in all. The young girl was right. But, here are at least five and perhaps six weeks, I dare not stop to count which, that I have already been in this prison of Bicêtre, and it seems to me that three days ago was Thursday.

Chapter IX

I have just made my will. And yet what is the use? I am con-demned at great cost, and all that I have will scarcely suffice to settle it. The guillotine is very expensive.

I leave a mother, a wife, and one child. A little girl, three years old, sweet, rosy, and frail, with great black eyes and long, nut-brown hair.

She was two years and one month old when I last saw her.

So, after my death, there will be three women, without a son, a husband, and a father; three orphans, so to speak; three wid-ows in point of law.

I admit that I am justly punished; but what have these inno-cent ones done?

No matter, they are disgraced, ruined; this is justice.

It is not my poor old mother who troubles me; she will die—or, if she lasts a few days longer, if up to the last moment she has a few warm coals in her stove, she will say nothing.

Nor is it my wife who troubles me; she is already weak and in poor health; she will die too.

I hope she will not go mad. They say that that makes one live; but at least the mind does not suffer; it sleeps and is as if it were dead.

But my daughter, my child, my poor little Marie, who laughs and plays, who is singing even now, and thinking of nothing. Ah! it is this that hurts me!

Chapter X

My cell consists of this:

Eight square feet and four walls of freestone at right angles to a flag-stone floor, which is raised one step above the outer cor-ridor.

To the right of the door, upon entering, is a sort of recess, a parody on an alcove. Here they have thrown a bit of straw on which the prisoner is supposed to rest and sleep, covered with a pair of linen trousers and a coat of ticking, the same, winter and summer.

Above my head, instead of the sky, is a black vault,—an *ogive*, it is called—from which hang thick cobwebs like rags.

For the rest, there are no windows, not even a vent-hole; and the one wooden door is entirely covered with iron.

No, I am wrong; in the centre of the door, toward the top, there is an opening, nine thumbs in width, cut out in the shape of a cross, and which at night is closed by the jailer.

Outside, is a long corridor, lighted and aired by means of narrow vent-holes near the ceiling, and divided into stone compartments, which open into one another by a series of low, arched doors; each compartment serves as some sort of an antechamber to a cell like mine. In these cells are the criminals sentenced by the director of the prison to severe discipline. The first three cells are reserved for those condemned to die, because, being nearer the jail, they are more convenient for the jailer. These cells are all that is left of the ancient château of Bicêtre, as it was built in the fifteenth century by the Cardinal of Winchester. He was the one who ordered Jeanne d'Arc burned. I heard this from some *visitors* who came to see me the other day in my cell, and who looked at me from a distance as though I were a beast in a menagerie. They gave the jailer a hundred sous for admitting them.

I forgot to say that day and night there is a gendarme at the door of my cell, and that I cannot raise my eyes to the square hole without always finding his, wide open, and staring at me.

People suppose that there are air and light in this stone box.

Chapter XI

Since it was not yet daylight, I was wondering what I should do with the night, when all at once an idea came into my mind. I rose and turned my lamp upon the four walls of my cell. They are covered with names, scrawls, and strange figures, one running into the other. It seems as though each convict wanted to leave a mark behind him here, at least. They are in pencil, chalk, charcoal, black, white, and gray, and often are cut deep into the stone, while here and there are rusty marks that might have been written with blood. Surely, were my mind clear, I would take much interest in this strange book which is developing, page after page, before my eyes on every stone of my cell. I should like to gather all these fragmentary thoughts together that are scattered over the stones, and find the owner under every name, and give life and feeling to these worn-out inscriptions, these broken sentences, these mangled words, these bodies without heads, like those who wrote them.

At the head of my bed are two burning hearts pierced by an arrow, and above are written the words: "*Love for life.*" The unfortunate writer did not make a long engagement.

By the side of this is a three-cornered hat with a small figure roughly sketched above it, and these words: "Long live the Emperor! 1824."

More burning hearts, with the inscription, a characteristic one in a prison: "*I love and adore Matthew Danvin.* JACQUES."

On the opposite wall is: "*Papavoine.*" The capital P is embellished with arabesques, and is carefully drawn.

A stanza of an obscene song.

A liberty-cap cut deep into the stone, with this below: "*Bories.—The Republic.*" He was one of the four sub-officers of La Rochelle. Poor fellow! How hideous are their imaginary political needs! For an idea, a dream, a thought, to meet this dread reality called the guillotine! And I am complaining, I, a wretch who has committed a real crime, who has spilled blood!

I shall look no further among the inscriptions. I have jut seen, in white crayon in the corner of the wall, a frightful picture,— the picture of the scaffold which perhaps is being built even now for me. The lamp just escaped falling from my hands.

Chapter XII

I sat down hurriedly on my straw, and my head fell forward upon my knees. But as soon as my childish terror had passed away I felt a strange curiosity to look again along the wall. Next to the name of Papavoine I removed a huge spider-web, thick with dust, from a corner of the wall. Behind the web were four or five names which were perfectly legible, and several others of which only a faint impression remained: "Dautun, 1815; Paulain, 1818; Jean Martin, 1821; Castaing, 1823." As I read these names I remembered the sad fate of each. Dautun cut his brother into pieces, and one night threw the head into a fountain and the body into a sewer in Paris. Poulain murdered his wife. Jean Martin shot his father as the old man was opening a window. Castaing, the physician, poisoned his friend; and instead of trying to cure him, as he pretended to do, he gave him more poison. Near to these was Papavoine, the dreadful madman who killed children by cutting open their heads.

A hot shiver went through me. These are the ones, I thought to myself, who have occupied my cell before me. Here, on the very floor on which I am standing, they thought their last thoughts, these bloody murderers! In this very dungeon, within these very walls, their last steps turned back and forth like a wild beast. Others took their places without delay; it seems that the cell is never empty. They left the place warm, and it is to me they left it. I, in turn, shall follow them to Clamart Cemetery, where the grass is always green.

I am neither visionary nor superstitious; perhaps these thoughts are making me feverish, but while I was thinking of them, it seemed to me all at once that these fatal names were written in lines of fire on the dark wall. A wild ringing was in my ears, a red glare came before my eyes; and then it seemed as though the dungeon were full of men, strange men, who carried their heads in their left hands, and held their hands between their teeth, for they had no hair. All shook their fists at me, except the parricide.

I closed my eyes in horror, but they all came before me still more distinctly.

Whether it was a dream, a vision, or a reality, I should have gone mad if a sudden thought had not dispelled them. I was on the point of falling when I felt crawling over my bare foot, a cold body with hairy legs; it was the spider whose web I had torn down.

That brought me back to myself. Oh, the frightful spectres! No, it was all a phantom, an idea of my empty and tortured brain. A fancy like Macbeth's! The dead are dead,—those who have been here, at least. They are safely locked within the tomb. It is not a prison from which one can escape. How could I have been so terrified? The door of the tomb does not open from within.

Chapter XIII

A few days ago I saw a horrible sight.

It happened before daylight. The prison was very noisy. I heard the opening and closing of the heavy gates, the turning of the locks and the iron bolts, the clank of the heavy bunches of keys hanging from the jailers' waists, the stairs creaking from top to bottom beneath hurried steps, and voices calling and answering from one end of the long corridors to the other. My neighbors in the cell of correction were more gay than usual. All Bicêtre seemed to be laughing, singing, running, and dancing.

I, the only quiet one in all this hubbub, the only still being in all the uproar, sat wondering and on the alert, listening to every sound.

A jailer passed.

I ventured to call and ask him if there was a *fête* going on in the prison.

"You may call it a *fête* if you like!" he replied. "To-day they are going to put the irons on the convicts who start to-morrow for Toulon. Do you want to see them? It will amuse you."

A show of any kind, however disagreeable, was a lucky thing for a solitary prisoner, and I accepted the fellow's offer.

The jailer took the usual precautions, to make sure of me, and then led me into a small empty cell, which contained not an article of furniture. It had a grated window, but a real window nevertheless, breast-high, and from which the real sky was visible.

"Here," said he, "you can see and hear. You will be alone in your box, like a king."

He went out, drawing after him the locks, bolts, and bars.

The window looked out upon a good-sized square court, around the four sides of which, like a wall, rose a great stone structure six stories high. Nothing could be more disagreeable, more forlorn, nor more wretched-looking than that façade with its many barred gratings, behind which peered out, above and below, a crowd of thin, white faces, one over the other, like the stones in a wall, and all framed, as it were, between the iron bars. They were the prisoners, watching the ceremony in which some day they were to take part. They looked like souls who were undergoing the punishment of purgatory, on their way to hell.

They were watching in silence the empty court. They were waiting. Among the tired, heavy faces, here and there shone out wild, piercing eyes, like sparks of fire.

The prison which surrounded the four sides of the square was not an unbroken wall. One of the four sides (the one looking to the east) was separated near the centre, and was connected to the other part by an iron railing. This railing opened on to a second court, smaller than the first, and, like it, flanked with walls full of black holes.

Around the walls of the main court were placed stone benches. In the centre was an iron pole for holding a lantern.

Noon struck. A large *porte-cochère* hidden behind a projection was suddenly opened. A wagon appeared, escorted by a species of dirty and shamefaced-looking soldiers in blue uniforms, with red epaulets and yellow shoulder-straps. It dragged

heavily across the court with the noise of grating iron. It contained the *chiourme* (the galley-slaves) and the chains.

At the same instant, as though that sound had roused every
other, the spectators at the windows, who, until then, had stood
still and silent, burst out into joyful cries and songs and threats
and imprecations, mingled with shouts of laughter, painful to
hear. They looked and acted like devils. A grin was on every
face, every fist was thrust through the bars, every voice cried
out, every eye flamed. I was startled to see such sparks bursting
out from the cinders. The keepers, among whom I recognized
from their fresh clothes and their apparent fright some curious
visitors from Paris, went calmly on with their work. One jumped
into the wagon, and threw out the chains, travelling-collars, and
bundles of linen trousers. Then they divided the work. Some
went to a corner of the court, and unwound the long chains,
which, in their slang, are called *the strings;* others spread out on
the pavement *the taffetas,* the shirts and trousers; the wisest,
under the eye of their captain, a short, thickset old man, exam-
ined the iron collars, which they tested still further by throwing
them upon the pavement. All this went on under the derisive
shouts of the prisoners, and the loud laughter of the convicts for
whom it was done, and who were lined up behind the gratings
of the old prison, which looked out upon the small court.

When these preliminaries were over, a gentleman with silver
embroidery on his coat, whom they called *the inspector,* gave an
order to the director of the prison; and a moment later, from
two or three of the lower doors, there poured out all at once into
the court, like a cloud of smoke, hideous crowds of ragged,
shouting men. These were the convicts.

At sight of them, the clamor at the windows increased. Some
of those who bore great names were welcomed with cries and
shouts, which they received with a sort of proud modesty. The
most of them wore caps which they had themselves woven from
the straw in their cells, of so curious a shape that those who
wore them could not fail to be noticed. One in particular
aroused shouts of enthusiasm,—a young man, perhaps seventeen years of age, with a face as smooth as a girl's. He came out
of his cell where he had been for a week. He had made a gar-

ment out of straw, which covered him from head to foot; and he sprang into the court, rolling over and over, with the agility of a serpent. He was a juggler, convicted of theft. There was a burst of handclapping and shouts of joy. The galley-slaves answered it, and the exchange of gayety between the real convicts and the candidates was frightful. Society, represented by the jailers and the frightened visitors, was of small account there; crime laughed in its very face, and made a family *fête* of this frightful punishment.

As each convict came out, he was led between two lines of gendarmes to the barred court, where he waited for the visit of the physicians. It was at this point that each tried a last resort in order to escape the journey, offering as an excuse their health, poor eyesight, lameness, or a maimed hand. But almost all were found fitted for work; and each resigned himself carelessly, for-getting a few minutes after, his pretended life infirmity.

The grating of the small court opened. A guard called the roll alphabetically; and then each convict came out, one by one, and took his stand in a corner of the large court, next to a comrade whose initial letter happened to be the same. Thus each was alone, carrying his own chain, side by side with a stranger; and if a convict chanced to be near a friend, the chain separated them. This was their greatest punishment.

When about thirty had gone out, the grating was closed. A keeper singled them out with his baton, threw in front of each a shirt, a jacket, and a pair of coarse linen trousers, then gave the signal, and they all began to undress. An unlooked-for incident changed this humiliation into torture.

Until then the weather had been clear; and although the October air was cold, every now and then the gray clouds opened, and from the chinks fell a ray of sunlight. But scarcely had the convicts dropped their prison-rags, and just as they stood naked before the suspicious glances of the keepers, and the curious looks of the strangers who walked around them in order to examine their shoulders, the sky became black, a cold autumn rain began to fall in torrents upon the square court, upon the bare heads and naked bodies of the galley-slaves, and upon their miserable clothes lying on the pavement.

In the twinkling of an eye the yard was cleared of everyone who was not a keeper or a galley-slave. The visitors from Paris sought shelter beneath the doorways.

The rain fell in torrents. Nothing could be seen in the court but the naked, dripping convicts on the soaked pavement. A moody silence had succeeded their boastful shouting. They shivered; their teeth chattered; their thin limbs and bent knees knocked against each other, and it was pitiful to see them putting over their blue bodies the shirts, jackets, and trousers which were soaked with the rain. They would better have remained naked.

One old man, however, was still lively. He cried out, wringing his dripping shirt, that *"this was not on the programme"*; then he began to laugh, shaking his fist at the sky.

When they had put on their travelling-clothes, they were led in groups of twenty or thirty to the other corner of the yard, where the cordons awaited them. These cordons are great long chains crossed every two feet by other shorter chains, at the end of which is attached a square collar which opens by means of a hinge fastened to one of the corners, and closes at the opposite corner by an iron bolt, locked on the galley-slave's neck throughout the entire journey. As these cordons lie on the ground they look like the backbone of a fish.

They made the slaves sit down in the mud on the soaking pavements. They tried on the collars; then two of the prison blacksmiths brought portable anvils, and riveted them on with a great iron hammer. It was a dreadful moment, and the bravest paled. At every stroke of the hammer upon the anvil, which leaned against their back, the victim's chin rebounded; the least movement made his head jump like a nutshell.

After this was done the convicts became gloomy. Nothing was heard but the clanking of the chains, an occasional groan, and the dull thud of the keeper's baton on the limbs of the offender. Some cried; the old men shivered and bit their lips. I looked with terror upon all these sinister profiles in their iron frames.

After the visit of the physicians, came that of the jailers; and after the jailers, the putting into chains. Three acts to the play!

A ray of sunlight appeared. It acted like a touch of fire. The convicts rose with one accord. The five cordons took hold of hands, and all together they formed an immense circle about the lantern-pole. My eyes grew weary watching them turn. They sang a prison-song, a slangy romance, to a tune now sad, now wild and gay. Every now and then shrill cries were heard and bursts of hoarse, breathless laughter, mingled with strange words; then furious shouts rang out, the clanking chains serving as an orchestra to the song, which was harsher than their grating. If ever I wanted a picture of a nocturnal meeting of witches I should ask for nothing better or worse than this.

A large tub was brought into the yard. The keeper stopped the dance with his baton, and led the convicts to this tub, in which some herbs were floating in a dirty, smoky, liquid. They began to eat.

When they had finished, they threw upon the pavement what was left of their soup and brown bread, and began to dance and sing again. It seems that this privilege is allowed them on this day and the following night.

I was watching the strange sight with such a hungry, trembling, close attention, that I had forgotten myself. A great pity filled me, and their laughter made me weep.

Suddenly, in the midst of my deep revery I saw the shouting circle stop and grow silent. Then every eye turned toward my window.

"The condemned man! The condemned man!" they cried, shaking their fingers; and the bursts of laughter increased.

I stood petrified.

I had no idea where they had seen me before or how they recognized me.

"Good-morning! Good-evening!" they cried, with their horrible chuckle. One of the youngest who was condemned to the galleys gave me a dull look of envy, and exclaimed: "He is happy! He will be *cut off!* (beheaded!) Farewell, comrade!"

I cannot describe my feelings. I was their comrade, in truth. La Grève is sister to Toulon. I was even on a lower level than they; they did me an honor. I shivered.

Yes, their comrade! And in a few days I, too, might be an amusing sight for them.

I was standing at the window, immovable, petrified, paralyzed; but when I saw the five cordons rush toward me with words of infernal good-fellowship, when I heard the frightful clanking of their chains, their shouts, their steps at the foot of the wall, it seemed as though this crowd of demons were climbing into my wretched cell. I gave a shriek, and hurled myself against the door with force enough to break it. No means of escape; the locks were drawn on the outside. I yelled, I shouted in fury. Then I seemed to hear the convicts' fearful voices coming nearer. I thought that their hideous faces were already at my window; I gave a second agonizing cry, and fell senseless to the floor.

Chapter XIV

When I recovered consciousness it was night. I was on a pallet; a lantern threw a flickering light on the ceiling, and I saw rows of other pallets on both sides of mine. I knew that I was in the hospital. For a moment I lay awake, but without thinking of anything, entirely given up to the joy of being in a bed. Once, this hospital and prison-cot would have made me shudder in disgust and pity; but I was no longer the same man. To be sure, the sheets were soiled and coarse to the touch, and the covering thin and ragged. I felt the boards beneath the mattress; but what of that? My limbs could stretch out between the rough sheets; and beneath the covering, thin as it was, I felt that horrible cold in my bones slowly beginning to disappear. I fell asleep again.

I was awakened by a great uproar; it was daybreak. The noise came from without. My bed was by the side of a window, and I rose to see what was happening.

The window looked out upon the great court of Bicêtre, which was filled with people; two lines of veterans had all they could do to make a narrow path across the court in the midst of the crowd.

Between this double line of soldiers, five long wagons full of men were jogging slowly along, jostling over each stone. They were the convicts who were leaving.

The wagons were uncovered. Each cordon occupied one. The convicts were seated sidewise on the benches, one leaning against the other, separated by their common chain, which lay along the entire length of the wagon, at the end of which stood a keeper, gun in hand. The clanking of the irons could be heard; and at every shake of the wagon, their heads were jerked forward and their dangling legs shook.

A fine, thin rain was falling, making the air frigid, and causing their gray linen trousers, which were already black, to cling to their knees. The rain poured from their long beards and short hair, their faces were purple; they were shivering, and their teeth chattered with rage and cold. More than this, they could not move. Once riveted within the chain, one is no longer anything but a part of that hideous cordon which moves like one man. The intellect leaves one; the prison-collar condemns it to death; and as to the being himself, he has no longer desires and an appetite except at fixed hours. So, motionless, the most of them half-naked, with bare heads and dangling feet, they began their journey of twenty-five days, seated in the same wagons, and dressed in the same clothes under the perpendicular sun of July as in the cold rains of November. One might say that in their office of hangmen, men wish the climate to do half.

Some sort of a horrible harangue arose between the people and those in the wagons,—abuse on the one side, bravado on the other, curses on both; but at a sign from the captain, I saw blows raining from the baton upon the wagons, on shoulders and heads alike, and everything assumed that exterior calm called *order*. But the wretches' eyes were full of vengeance, and their fists were clinched on their knees.

The five wagons, guarded by mounted gendarmes and keepers on foot, disappeared one after another beneath the high arched gate of Bicêtre; a sixth followed, in which the kettles, brass porringers, and extra chains rattled together in noisy confusion. Some keepers who had been detained at the canteen ran out to catch up with their squad. The crowd began to scatter. The picture vanished like a phantasmagoria. By degrees, the heavy rolling of the wheels and the tramp of the horses' hoofs on the paved road from Fontainebleau grew faint, and the crack of the whips, the clank of the chains, and the cries of the people wishing the galleys an unlucky journey, died away.

But for them it was only the beginning!

What was it the lawyer said to me? The galleys! Ah, yes! death a thousand times,—the scaffold rather than the galleys; nothing rather than hell. I would give my neck to the knife of the guillotine, but not to the prison-collar! The galleys, just Heaven!

Chapter XV

Unfortunately I was not ill, and the next day I had to leave the hospital and return to my cell.

Not ill! Ah no, I am young, strong, and healthy. The blood runs freely in my veins; my every member answers my every fancy. I am strong in mind and body, I was made to live long; yes, this is all true, and yet I have a malady,—a mortal malady, a malady made by the hand of man.

Since I came from the hospital, the idea has come to me to become mad; perhaps I might escape if I could do this. The doctors and the Sisters of Charity seemed to be interested in me. To die so young, and such a death! One would have thought they were sorry for me, they gathered so close about my pallet. Bah! it was from curiosity. And then, these people who help you, cure you of a fever, but not of a death-sentence. Yet that would be so easy for them. An open door! What would it matter to them?

I have no chance now; my appeal will be rejected because everything is correct. The witnesses testified clearly; the plaintiffs have pleaded well; the judges have sentenced. I do not expect—but—no; what folly! There is no more hope. The appeal is a rope which holds you suspended above an abyss, and which creaks every moment until it breaks. It is as if the knife of the guillotine took six weeks to fall.

Suppose I were pardoned?—Pardoned! And by whom? And why? And how? It is not possible for them to pardon me. It is for an *example*, as they say.

Only three steps remain for me,—Bicêtre, the Conciergerie, La Grève.

Chapter XVI

During the few hours that I spent in the hospital I sat near a window in the sunshine,—it had come out again,—or at least in as much of it as could creep in through the grating.

I sat there, with my heavy head in my hands, which was more than they could hold, my elbows on my knees, and my feet on the rounds of my chair, for I am so weak that I lean over as though I no longer had either bones in my limbs or muscles in my flesh.

The close air of the prison was worse than ever; my ears still rang with the noise of the galleys' chains, and I was growing very tired of Bicêtre. It seemed to me that God ought to pity me, that he might at least send me a little bird to sing to me from the edge of the opposite roof.

I do not know whether it was God or the Devil who answered my wish, but almost at that very moment I heard a voice beneath my window; not that of a bird, but, what was better, the pure, fresh, clear voice of a young girl of fifteen. I raised my head with a start, and listened greedily to the song she sung. The air was slow and languishing, a kind of sad and lamentable cooing. The words were something like these:—

> "It was in the Rue du Mail
> I was caught, oh, sorry tale!
> Wretched I!
> By three gendarmes, cruel men,
> Who came rushing at me when
> I passed by."

I cannot tell you how bitter was my disappointment. The voice sang on:—

> "They came rushing at me, so!
> Put great handcuffs on me, oh!

Such a load.
Then arrived the police-spy,
And a robber-friend came by
    On the road,

A friend both quick and rife [nimble].
And I cried: 'Go tell my wife
    I am caught!'
Then my wife came with a run,
'Husband, tell me, what hast done?'
    (Thus she fought.)

Thus my wife in rage began,
And I said: 'I've killed a man
    Oh, my dear!
His gold watch and money too,
And his rings so bright and new,
    I have here!

'Yes, his rings so new and bright!'
My poor wife set out that night
    For Versailles;
A petition she did bring
For my pardon; begged the king,
    With a cry!

Sought the king to plead my cause.
And had I escaped the laws,
    Wretched I,
I would deck my wife, I say,
In rich silks, and ribbons gay
    I would buy.

Slippers, too, I'd have her wear;
But the king in wrath did swear:
    'By my crown!
I will make him dance a dance
O'er a floorless, broad expanse,
    Dangling down!'"

I could hear no more, nor did I wish to. The half-veiled meaning of the horrible complaint; the struggle of the brigand with the sentinel; the robber he meets and sends to his wife with the horrible message: "I have killed a man, and have been arrested," *"I have made an oak-tree sweat, and I am caught;"* the woman running to Versailles with a petition, and his *Majesty* growing indignant and threatening the accused to make him dance *the dance where there is no floor,*—all this sung to the sweetest tune in the sweetest voice human ear ever heard! I was amazed, petrified, completely broken down. It was so dreadful that all these terrible words should come from such fresh and rosy lips. It was like drivel from a slug on a rose.

I cannot describe my feelings; I was both ashamed and sorry. The *patois* of the prison and the galleys, such strange and bloody language, such hideous slang, sung by a young girl, in a voice that was a graceful combination of a child's and a woman's! All these deformed, shapeless words sung with such delicacy and rhythm.

Ah, what an infamous place a prison is! There is a poison about it which spoils everything. Everything is tarnished by it, even the song of a young girl of fifteen. You find a bird there; it has mud on its wing: you gather a pretty flower, you smell it; its odor is offensive.

Chapter XVII

Oh, if I could only escape, how I would run!

But no, one should not run. That would rouse suspicion. One should walk slowly, and sing, with head erect. If possible, one should wear an old blue smock-frock with red figures on it. That would be a good disguise. Every gardener in the neighborhood wears one.

I know a thicket near Arcueil, by the side of a swamp, where I used to come with the fellows every Thursday when I was at college, to fish for frogs. I would hide there until evening.

When night came I would go on again. I would go to Vincennes. No; the river would prevent me. I would go to Arpajon. It might be better to go by Saint-Germain, to Havre, and embark for England.

Well, in any case, I would finally reach Longjumeau. A gendarme passes me. He asks for my passport. I am lost!

Ah, poor dreamer! first break the three feet of thick wall which holds you a prisoner! Death! Death!

And to think that once when I was a child I came here to Bicêtre, to see the great dungeons and the madmen!

Chapter XVIII

While I have been writing all this, my lamp has grown dim, daylight has come, the chapel clock has struck six—

What does that mean? My keeper has just been into my cell; he took off his cap, bowed to me, apologized for disturbing me, and asked me in as mild a tone as his tough voice could command, what I wanted for breakfast.

I began to shiver. Will it happen to-day?

Chapter XIX

Yes, it is going to happen to-day!

The director of the prison came himself to see me. He asked me what he could do for me. He hoped I had nothing to complain of, either in regard to him or his subordinates; asked with interest about my health, and how I had passed the night. As he was leaving, he called me *sir!*

It is to happen to-day!

Chapter XX

This jailer thinks I have no complaint to make of him or his subordinates, and he is right. It would be wrong indeed of me to complain; they have done their duty in guarding me carefully;

and they have been polite at all times. Should I not be content?

This good jailer, with his gentle smile and kind words, his eye which flatters and at the same time spies, his great thick hands,—he is the prison incarnate; he is Bicêtre personified. Everything is a prison about me. I find it in every form; under the human form as under that of lock and key. This wall is the prison in stone; this door is the prison in wood; the keepers are prisons in flesh and bone. The prison is a horrible being, complete, indivisible,—half-house, half-man. I am its prey: it broods over me; it holds me in its close embrace; it encloses me within its granite walls, clasps me beneath its iron bolts, and watches me with its jailer's eyes.

Ah, wretch that I am! what shall I become? What do they want to do with me?

Chapter XXI

I am calm now. All is well over. I have recovered from the horrible anxiety which the director's visit gave me. For, I will confess, I did have hope. Now, thank God, I have none.

This is what has just taken place:—

Just as the clock struck half-past six—no, a quarter-past—my prison door opened. An old man with white hair, in a long brown cloak, entered. His cloak was thrown back, and I saw a cassock and a band. He was a priest.

But he was not the prison chaplain, and this did not augur well.

He sat down opposite me, and smiled kindly; then he bowed his head, and raised his eyes to heaven,—that is, to the ceiling of my cell. I understood what he meant.

"My son," said he, "are you prepared?"

I answered in a weak voice,—

"I am not prepared, but I am ready."

A mist rose before my eyes, an icy perspiration came out all over me; I felt my temples swelling and my ears ringing.

While I swayed in my chair as though half asleep, the good man talked to me.

At least, I think he did; I seem to remember that his lips moved; and, while his hands clasped each other, his eyes lighted up.

The door opened a second time. The grating of the key roused me from my stupor and him from his discourse. A gentleman in black, accompanied by the director of the prison, appeared, and bowed low to me. The man wore on his face that sad official look which belongs to undertakers. He held a roll of paper in his hand.

"Monsieur," he said with a courteous smile, "I am the bailiff from the royal court-house of Paris. I have the honor to bring you a message from the attorney-general."

The first shock over, all my presence of mind returned.

"Is it the attorney-general," I asked, "who demands my head? I feel highly honored that he has written to me. I trust that my death will give him much pleasure; for it would be hard to think that he asked for it so anxiously, and that after all it was indifferent to him."

I said all this, and continued in a firm voice,—

"Read it, sir."

He began to read a long document, chanting at the end of every line, and hesitating between each word. It was the refusal of my appeal.

"The sentence will be carried out to-day, on the Place de Grève," he added, when he had finished, and without raising his eyes from the paper. "We leave at exactly half-past seven for the Conciergerie. My dear sir, will you be good enough to be ready?"

I had heard nothing for a moment or two. The director was talking with the priest, who was gazing at the paper. I glanced toward the half-open door. Ah, miserable fool! four soldiers stood in the corridor!

The bailiff repeated his question, this time looking at me.

"Whenever you please," I replied. "You may make your self easy." He bowed, saying,—

"I shall have the honor of returning for you in half an hour."

Then they left me alone.

O God! some means of escape! some means; I know not what! I must escape! I must! And at once! By the door, the window, through the timbers of the roof! Even though I leave my skin on the beams!

Oh, fury! demons! malediction! It would take mouths to pierce through the walls with the best of instruments, and I have not even a nail or an hour!

Chapter XXII

In the Conciergerie

HERE I AM TRANSFERRED, AS THE REPORT SAYS.
But the journey is worth describing.

The clock was striking half-past seven as the bailiff again presented himself at the door of my cell. "Monsieur," said he, "I am ready for you." Alas! he and others as well!

I rose and took one step forward; it seemed as though I could not take another, my head was so heavy and my limbs so weak. But after a moment I recovered myself, and walked with firm steps. Before leaving the cell, I cast a last glance at it. I loved it, that cell! Then I left it empty and open; a strange thing in a cell.

But it will not remain so very long. This evening they expect some one, the jailers said, a convict whom the Court of Assizes is sentencing even now.

At a turn of the corridor the priest joined us. He had just breakfasted.

As we left the jail, the director took me affectionately by the hand, and added four veterans to my escort.

Before the door of the hospital a dying old man cried out to me, "*Au revoir!*"

We reached the courtyard, where I breathed again; the air did me good.

We did not walk far, however.

A carriage drawn by post-horses was waiting in the first

court; it was the same that had brought me, a kind of long cabriolet, divided into two sections by a longitudinal grating of iron wire, so thick that it looked as if it might have been knitted. Each section had a door, one in front, the other at the rear of the cabriolet. The whole thing was so dirty, so black and dusty, that a hearse for paupers would be a king's chariot in comparison.

Before burying myself in this two-wheeled tomb, I glanced about the yard with a desperate look, before which the very walls might have crumbled. The court, a small square, planted with trees, was even fuller of spectators than it had been for the galleys. Already the crowd had begun!

As on the day of the departure of the galleys, a fine, icy rain was falling, which is coming down even now as I write, and which will probably continue all day, even after I am gone.

The roads were rough, the court-yard full of mud and water. I was glad to see the crowd standing in all this mud.

The bailiff and a gendarme stepped into the front compartment, the priest, a second gendarme, and myself into the other. There were four mounted gendarmes around the carriage. So, without the driver, there were eight men to one.

As I stepped in, an old woman with gray eyes exclaimed, "I like this even better than the galleys."

I understood what she meant. It was a sight that was more easily grasped and sooner over. It was just as pleasant, and more convenient. There is nothing to distract one. There is only one man, and on him alone is centred as much misery as on all the galleys together. Only it is less scattered; it is a concentrated liquor, and much sweeter.

The carriage began to move. It made a dull sound as it passed under the arch of the great entrance; then it turned into the avenue, and the dark walls of Bicêtre were lost behind us. As in a stupor I felt myself carried on, like a man in a lethargy, who knows that he is being buried, yet who can neither move nor cry. In a vague way I heard the jingling of the bells on the horses' necks, keeping time, and playing a sort of hiccough, the iron wheels moving over the pavement or grating against the carriage as it crossed the ruts in the road, the even galop of the gendarmes on either side of the carriage, and the lashing of the driver's whip. It all seemed like a whirlwind that was sweeping me away.

Through a hole in the wire grating opposite me, my eyes fell mechanically on the inscription engraved in large letters above the great door of Bicêtre: *"Hospital for the Aged."*

"Ah," I said to myself, "there are people who indeed grow old there."

And as happens between sleep and waking, I turned the idea over and over again in my mind, which was already dull with grief. All at once the carriage passed from the avenue into the highroad, and the point of view of my skylight was changed. The towers of Notre Dame arose blue and dim in the mist of Paris. Immediately the view-point of my mind changed also. I was a machine like the carriage. To the thought of Bicêtre now succeeded the thought of the towers of Notre Dame. "Those who are on the tower where the flag is have a fine view," I said to myself, smiling stupidly.

I think that it was at that moment that the priest began to speak. I patiently let him talk. The noise of the wheels, the gallop of the horses, the lash of the driver's whip, still were in my ears. The priest's words were only an extra noise.

So I listened in silence to the monotonous fall of words which lulled my mind like the murmur of a fountain, and which passed before me, always varied, yet always the same, like the gnarled elms along the highroad, when suddenly I was roused by the sharp, jerky voice of the bailiff.

"Well, Monsieur Abbé," said he, in a tone that sounded almost gay, "what news have you?"

He turned to the priest.

The latter continued talking to me, and made no reply. The noise of the carriage-wheels drowned the bailiff's words.

"Oh!" he continued, raising his voice above the noise of the carriage; "this infernal wagon!"

Infernal indeed!

He went on,—

"No doubt it is the joggling of the carriage that prevents his hearing me. What was I saying? Tell me what was I saying,

Monsieur Abbé? Oh, yes! Do you know the news of Paris to-day?"

I swayed, as though he were speaking of me.

"No," replied the priest, who finally heard; "I had no time to read the papers this morning. I shall see them this evening. When I am busy like this all day, I tell my porter to keep my papers, and I read them on my return."

"Bah!" resumed the bailiff, "you must know this. The news of Paris! the news of this morning!"

I spoke.

"I think I know it."

The bailiff looked at me.

"You! Indeed! In that case, what do you think of it?"

"You are curious!" I replied.

"And why, sir?" asked the bailiff. "Every one has his political opinion, and I esteem you too highly to think that you are without one. As for me, I am entirely of the opinion that the National Guard should be restored. I was sergeant of my company, and it was very pleasant."

I interrupted him.

"I did not know that this was the news."

"And what is it, then? You said you knew."

"I was referring to something else, in which Paris is interested to-day."

The stupid fellow did not understand, and his curiosity was roused.

"Something else? Where in the devil could you learn any news? What is it, my dear sir? Do you know what it is, Monsieur Abbé? Are you better informed than I? Tell me, I beg you. What is this news? You know I love news. I tell it to the President, and it amuses him."

And a thousand idle stories they are, too, that he tells. He turned first to the priest and then to me; but I only shrugged my shoulders.

"Well," said he, "of what are you thinking?"

"I think," I answered, "that I will not think any more this evening."

"Ah, yes, of course!" he replied. "But come! you are too sad! Monsieur Castaing talked."

Then, after a pause,—

"I escorted Monsieur Papavoine; he wore his otter cap, and smoked his cigar. As to the young fellows of La Rochelle, they talked only among themselves. But they talked."

Another pause; then he continued,—

"Fools! Enthusiasts! Apparently they scorned the whole world. But for what you have done, I find you very pensive, young man."

"'Young man,'" I cried; "I am older than you; and every fifteen minutes makes me a year older, besides."

He turned, looked at me a moment in stupid wonder, and then began to laugh loudly.

"Come! you are jesting, you older than I! I might well be your grandfather!"

"I am not jesting," I answered sadly.

He opened his tobacco pouch.

"Here, my dear sir, do not be angry; take a pinch of tobacco, and do not bear me ill-will."

"Do not fear; I shall not have long to bear it."

Just then his tobacco pouch, which he offered me, came in contact with the fire grating between us. A jolt of the carriage knocked it out of his hand, and it fell violently to the floor, at the gendarme's feet.

"Cursed grating!" cried the bailiff.

He turned to me.

"Am I not unfortunate? All my tobacco is lost!"

"I am losing more than you," I replied, smiling.

He tried to gather up the tobacco, muttering between his teeth,—

"More than I! That is easy to say! But no tobacco all the way to Paris! It's dreadful!"

The priest addressed a few consoling words to him; and, perhaps I was dreaming, but it seemed as though it were the conclusion of the exhortation, the beginning of which I had heard. By degrees the conversation was carried on only between the priest and the bailiff; I let them talk on their side, and gave myself up to my own thoughts on mine.

When we reached the city limits I was still preoccupied, no doubt, but Paris seemed noisier than ever.

The carriage stopped a moment at the toll-gate. The city custom-house officers came out to examine it. Had I been a sheep or an ox going to slaughter, they would have had a purse of silver thrown them; but a human head does not pay for right of way, and we passed on.

We crossed the Boulevard, and the cabriolet went at a rapid rate through the old winding streets of the Faubourg Saint-Marceau and La Cité, which twine and intertwine one about the other like the thousand paths of an ant-hill. On the pavement of these narrow streets the noise of the wheels became so loud that all other sounds were lost. When I glanced through the little square hole, it seemed that the crowd of passers-by had stopped to watch the carriage, and that groups of children were running after it. It seemed, too, as though now and then I saw on the cross-walks a ragged man or woman, sometimes both together, with a bundle of printed papers in their hands, that the people were quarrelling over, opening their mouths as though in the act of giving a loud cry.

The Palace clock struck half-past eight as we reached the court-yard of the Conciergerie. The sight of the wide staircase, the black chapel, the sinister-looking entrances, froze me; and when the carriage came to a stand-still, I thought the beating of my heart had stopped too.

But I gathered myself together. The gate was opened like lightning; I jumped from the cell-on-wheels, and was hurried at rapid strides beneath the arch, between two lines of soldiers. Already a great crowd had collected about me.

Chapter XXIII

As I walked along the public corridors of the Palais du Justice I felt at my ease and almost free; but all my resolution left me when they opened the low doors, the secret staircases, and the close and dark inner corridors, where no one enters except the prisoners or those who convict them.

The bailiff never left my side. The priest went away, to return in two hours; he had business to look after.

They took me to the director's office, where the bailiff left me. It was an exchange. The director begged him to wait an instant, saying that he had some *game* to give him which he might take at once to Bicêtre on the return of the carriage. Probably it is the man who was condemned to-day, and who, this evening, will lie on the straw which I had not the time to use.

"Very well," said the bailiff to the director. "I will wait a moment; we can make out both reports at the same time. That is a good plan."

Meanwhile I had been put into a small office opening out of that of the director. There I was left alone under lock and key.

I do not know of what I was thinking, nor how long I was there, when all at once a rough and loud burst of laughter roused me from my stupor.

I raised my eyes tremblingly. I was no longer alone in the cell. A man was there with me,—a man about fifty-five, of medium height, wrinkled, round-shouldered, grayish, and thick-set, with an evil look in his gray eyes, and a bitter smile on his lips; dirty, ragged, and half-naked, he was altogether a most repulsive sight.

The door must have opened, thrust him in, and closed again without my having noticed it. If only death might come in that way!

For a few seconds we looked at each other, that man and I,—he, with a laugh like a rattle; I, half-amazed, half-frightened.

"Who are you?" I asked at length.

"You have the right to ask," he replied; "I am a *friauche*."

"A *'friauche!'* What is that?"

The question seemed to augment his gayety.

"That," he answered, in the midst of a fresh burst of laughter, "that means that the *taule* will play with my *Sorbonne* in six weeks, as he is about to play with your body in six hours. Ah, ah! it seems that now you understand."

I was white; my hair stood on end. He was the other convict, whom they were expecting at Bicêtre,—my successor.

He continued,—

"What can you expect? I will tell you my story. I am the son of a good *peigre;* it is a pity that Charlot (the hangman) took the trouble once to tie his cravat. It was when the gallows reigned, by the grace of God. At the age of six, I had neither father nor mother. In the summer I rolled in the dust of the gutters, to see if some one would throw me a penny from the door of the stages; in the winter I went about in the mud with bare feet, blowing on my red fingers to keep them warm. My skin could be seen through my trousers. At the age of nine I had begun to use my hands; now and then I emptied a pocket or stole a cloak. At the age of ten I was a pickpocket. Then I made some acquaintances. At seventeen I was a thief. I forced open a shop by means of a false key. I was arrested. Being of age, I was sent to work in the galleys. It was hard there; sleeping on a plank, drinking nothing but water, eating black bread, dragging after me a stupid ball, which was of no use to any one, and suffering from burns from a baton, and from the hot sun too. Besides all this, we were shaved, and I had such beautiful brown hair. Well, no matter! I served my time. Fifteen years pass, after a while! I was thirty-two. One fine morning they gave me a ticket and sixty-six francs, which I had saved during the fifteen years in the galleys by working sixteen hours a day, thirty days a month, and twelve months a year. That was all right. I wanted to be an honest man with my sixty-six francs, and I had more beautiful ideas under my rags than there are under an abbé's cassock. But how the devils acted with that passport! It was yellow, and they had written on it 'Freed galley.' I had to show it everywhere, and present it every week before the mayor of the village where they compelled me to live. It was a fine recommendation! A galley! They were afraid of me; the children ran from me, and every door was shut in my face. No one would give me work. I devoured my sixty-six francs. I had to live. I showed that my arms were strong enough to work, but they shut their doors. I offered to do a day's

labor for fifteen sous, for ten, for five. No. So what was there left
for me to do? One day I was hungry. I knocked in a baker's case,
seized some bread, and the baker seized me. I did not eat the
bread; and I had the galleys for life, with three letters branded
on my shoulders. You may see them if you wish. They call this
act of justice *the second offence*. I was back again to the galleys.
They took me to Toulon; this time with the life convicts. I had
to escape. I had three walls to cut through, two chains to break,
and one nail with which to do it; but I succeeded. They shot
after me; for, like the cardinals at Rome, we were dressed in
scarlet, and they shoot when we leave. Their powder went to the
sparrows. This time I had no yellow passport, but no money
either. I met some fellows who had served their turn or broken
their chains. Their chief suggested that I join them; they committed murders on the great highways. I accepted his offer, and
set about killing in order to live. Now it was a stage-coach, now
a post-chaise, now a cattle-dealer on horseback. We took the
money, let the beast or the wagon go, and buried the man under
a tree, being careful that his feet did not stick out; then we
danced on the spot, so that the earth would not look as though
it had been freshly turned. I grew old in such pursuits, living in
the brush-wood, sleeping beneath the shining stars, and wandering from wood to wood, but at least I was free and my own
master. Every one has some object in life; it may as well be one
as another. But one starry night, the gendarmes seized us by our
collars. My comrades escaped; but I, the eldest, was caught in
the claws of these cats with their cockade hats. I was brought
here. Already I had mounted every step of the ladder except
one. To have stolen a handkerchief or murdered a man was all
the same to me once; there remained but one more *recidive* to
apply to me. I had only to reach the hangman. My trial was
short. I was beginning to grow old, and to be of no further use.
My father was hanged, and I am now about to enter the monas-
tery of Mont-à-Regret (the guillotine). There, comrade!"

I was speechless at his story. He began to laugh louder than
ever, and tried to take my hand, but I recoiled in horror.

"Friend," said he, "you do not look brave. Do not be a coward
in the face of death. It will be hard for a moment, when you

reach the Place de Grève, but it is so soon over with! I should like to be there to show you how to fall. A thousand gods! I would rather not make another appeal, if they would cut me down with you. The same priest would serve us both; it is all the same to me to take your leavings. You see that I am a good fellow. Hey? Will you accept my friendship?"

Again he started to approach me.

"Monsieur," I replied, pushing him away, "I thank you."

Fresh burst of laughter at my reply.

"Ah! ah! monsieur, you are a marquis! You are a marquis!"

I interrupted him.

"My friend, I have need to collect myself; leave me."

The serious tone in which I uttered the words sobered him at once. He nodded his gray and almost bald head; then imprinting his nails into his shaggy breast, which was bare under his open shirt, he murmured between his teeth,—

"Ah, I understand, the priest!"

After a few moments' silence,—

"Yes," he said, almost timidly, "you are a marquis; that is good. But you have a fine cloak which will not be of much use to you! The *taule* will take it. Give it to me; I will sell it, and buy tobacco."

I took off my cloak, and handed it to him. He began to clap his hands in childish glee. Then, seeing that I was in my shirt-sleeves and shivering, he exclaimed,—

"You are cold, sir; take this. It is raining, and you will get wet; besides, one must look decent in the wagon."

He removed his thick gray linen coat, and put my arms through it. I let him do so.

Then I leaned against the wall; but I cannot tell what effect the man had on me. He began to examine the cloak which I had given him, crying out every second with joy,—

"The pockets are perfectly new! The collar is not worn! I can get at least fifteen francs for it. What luck! Tobacco enough for my six weeks!"

The door opened. They had come for both of us,—to escort me to the room where the convicts awaited their turn; to take him to Bicêtre. He took his place, with a laugh, in the midst of the guard who was to lead him away, and said to the gendarmes,—

"Ah, do not be deceived! Monsieur and I have changed our coats, that is all; but do not mistake me for him. But the devil! that would not trouble me, now that I have some thing with which to get some tobacco!"

Chapter XXIV

The old criminal stole my cloak, for I did not give it to him; and he left me this ragged thing, this dirty coat. What do I look like?

I did not let him take my cloak from my feeling of indifference or charity. No; but because he was stronger than I. Had I refused, he would have struck me with his great fists.

Charity indeed! I was full of evil thoughts. I should have liked to strangle him with my hands, the old robber! and crush him beneath my feet!

I feel that my heart is full of rage and bitterness. I think that the sack of hatred has burst. Death makes one wicked.

Chapter XXV

They took me to a cell where there were only the four walls, many bars across the window, and many locks at the door, all of which goes without saying.

I asked for a table, a chair, and the necessary writing-materials, all of which they brought me.

Then I asked for a bed. The jailer looked at me in surprise, as though to ask, "Of what use?"

But they put up a cot in the corner. At the same time a gendarme was stationed in what they called "my room." Were they afraid I would strangle myself with the mattress?

Chapter XXVI

It is ten o'clock.

O my poor little girl! only six hours, and I shall be dead! I shall be an unclean something which is dragged over the cold table of the amphitheatres,—a head that they will east on one side, a body that they will dissect on the other; then what is left on one side they will put into a coffin, and take to Clamart.

This is what they are going to do with your father, these men who do not hate me, but who pity me, and who could save me. They want to kill me. Do you understand all this, Marie? Kill me in cold blood, systematically, for the good of the thing. Ah, my God!

Poor little maid! Your father who loved you so, your father who kissed your sweet little white neck, who ran his hand through your curls as through silk, who took your sweet, round face in his hands, who jumped you on his knees, and at night joined your little hands to pray to God!

Who is there now who will do all this for you? Who is there to love you? All the children of your age will have fathers except you. How can you, my child, give up, on New Year's Day, the gifts, the pretty playthings, the candies, and kisses? How can you, poor little orphan, give up drinking and eating?

Oh, if the jury had only seen my little Marie, they would have understood that they must not kill the father of a baby three years old!

And when she grows up, if she lives, what will become of her? Her father will be one of the souvenirs of the people of Paris. She will blush for me and my name; she will be scorned, repulsed, despised, on account of me—me, who loves her with my whole heart. O my beloved little Marie! Is it really true that you will feel shame and horror for me?

Miserable wretch! what a crime I have committed, and what a crime I am about to make society commit!

Oh, is it really true that I am going to die before the close of the day? Is it really true that it is I? Yes, this dull sound of cries which I hear outside, this crowd of joyous people who are already running to the wharves, the gendarmes who are getting themselves ready in their barracks, the priest in his black gown, the other man with the red hands,—it is all for me! It is I who am going to die! I, this very I who am here, who am living, moving, and breathing, who is seated at this table, which is like another table, and might be elsewhere. It is I, whom I touch and feel, and whose clothing makes these folds!

Chapter XXVII

If only I knew how it was done, and in what way they died there; but it is horrible, because I do not know.

The name of the thing is frightful, and I do not understand how I ever could have written or pronounced it.

The combination of those ten letters, their shape, their appearance, may well arouse a frightful idea. The physician of evil who invented the thing had a predestined name.

The picture which this hideous word brings before me is vague, indistinct, and sinister. Every syllable is like a part of the machine. In my mind I build and overthrow the monstrous scaffold unceasingly.

I dare not ask a question; but it is frightful not to know what it is, or how it works. It seems that there is a seesaw, and that you lie down on your stomach. Ah! my hair will turn white before my head falls!

Chapter XXVIII

But once I saw it.

I was driving over the Place de Grève one day, about eleven o'clock in the morning. All at once the carriage stopped.

There was a crowd on the Place. I put my head out of the window. Crowds filled La Grève and the wharf; and men, women, and children were standing on the parapet. Above the heads I saw a kind of platform of red wood, that three men were erecting.

A convict was to be executed that very day, and they were building the machine.

I turned my head aside before I saw any more. Beside my carriage a woman said to a child,—

"See! look! the knife works badly; they are going to oil the groove with candle-grease."

That is probably what they are doing to-day. Eleven o'clock has just struck. No doubt they are oiling the groove.

Ah, this time, wretch that I am, I shall not turn aside my head!

Chapter XXIX

Oh, my pardon! my pardon! Perhaps they will pardon me. The king bears me no ill-will. Let them find my lawyer! quick, my lawyer! I want the galleys. Five years in the galleys, and let it all end, or twenty years—or life with the crimson brand. But pardon for my life!

A criminal can still walk; he can come and go; he can see the sun.

Chapter XXX

The priest has returned.

He has white hair, a quiet manner, and a kind and gentle face; he is a good and charitable man. This morning I saw him empty his purse into the hands of the prisoners. How does it happen that his voice has nothing which may move or be moved? How does it happen that he has not told me anything which appealed to my heart or my mind?

This morning my thoughts were wandering. I scarcely heard what he said to me. But his words seemed useless, and

I was indifferent; they fell like the cold rain on that icy window.

But when he came in just now, the sight of him did me good. Among all these men, he alone is still a man for me, I say to myself. And he gave me a great thirst for good and consoling words.

We sat down, he on the chair, I on the bed. He said to me, "My son." This word opened my heart. He continued:—

"My son, do you believe in God?"

"Yes, my father," I answered.

"Do you believe in the holy Catholic, Apostolic, and Roman Church?"

"Yes," I replied.

"My son," he continued, "you seem by your manner to doubt."

Then he began to speak. He talked a long time; he used many words. When he thought he had finished, he rose and looked at me for the first time since the beginning of his discourse.

"Well?" he asked.

I declare that I listened to him first with eagerness, then with attention, then with devotion.

I rose too.

"Monsieur," I replied, "leave me alone, I beg."

"When shall I return?" he asked.

"I will let you know."

Then he went out without a word, but shaking his head as though saying,—

"An unbeliever!"

But no, low as I may have fallen, I am not that; God is my witness that I believe in him. But what did the old man say to me? Nothing which roused any feeling, any tenderness, any tears; nothing from *the soul;* nothing which came straight from his heart into mine; nothing which came from him to me. On the contrary, something vague, indistinct, applicable to everything and everybody; emphatic where there was need for depth, dull where it should have been simple,—a kind of sentimental sermon and theological elegy. Here and there a Latin quotation in Latin. Saint Augustine, Saint Gregory—what do I care about them? And then he seemed to be reciting a lesson which he had recited twenty times already, or of repeating a theme which was almost worn out from having been so long in his mind. There was no expression in his eyes, no feeling in his voice, no meaning in his gestures.

Yet how could it be otherwise? This priest is the official chaplain of the prison. His mission is to console and exhort, and he lives on this. The galleys, the victims, are the resource of his eloquence. He confesses and attends them, because he has his position to fill. He has grown old in leading men to death. For a long time he has been accustomed to that before which others tremble. His locks, well powdered with white, no longer stand on end; the galleys and the scaffold are everyday affairs for him. He is *blasé*. Probably he has his copybook,—such a page for the galleys; such a page for the convict condemned to die. He is told the evening before, that there will be some one for him to console at such an hour the next day. He asks who it is, galley or convict, and re-reads the page; then he makes his visit. In this way it happens that those who are bound for Toulon and those who are to go to La Grève are common ground for him, and he for them.

Oh, if instead of all this they would send me some young vicar, or an old curate in charge of his first parish; if they would go to him in the corner of his fireplace, where he is reading his book and expecting nothing, and say to him:—

"There is a man who is about to die, and you are the one who must console him. You must be there when they bind his hands, when they cut off his hair; you must enter the wagon with him, and with your crucifix hide the hangman from him; you must be jostled with him over the pavement to La Grève; you must go with him through the horrible crowd, drunk with blood; you must embrace him at the foot of the scaffold; you must stay there until his head is severed from his body."

And when they brought him to me, trembling, and shivering from head to foot, I would throw myself into his arms, and at his feet; and he would cry, and we would cry together, and he would grow eloquent, and I would be consoled; my heart would unburden itself against his, and he would take my soul, and I would take his God.

But this good old man,—what is he to me, or I to him? An unhappy individual, a shadow, like many another he has already seen—a unit to add to the number of executions.

Perhaps I am wrong thus to repel him; it is he who is good, and I who am bad. Alas! it is not my fault. It is the atmosphere of the prison which spoils and kills everything.

They have just brought me some food; they thought that I must be in need of it. The tray is neat and dainty; and there is a chicken, I think, besides other things. Well! I tried to eat; but at the first bite everything fell from my mouth, it tasted so bitter and nauseating!

Chapter XXXI

A man just came in, with his hat on his head; but he scarcely noticed me. He opened a foot-rule, and began to measure the height of the stones in the wall, speaking in a very loud voice, and saying, *"That is right;"* or, *"That is not right."*

I asked the gendarme who he was. It seems that he is an under-architect employed in the prison.

On his part, his curiosity was aroused concerning me. He exchanged a few words in a low tone with the jailers who accompanied him, looked at me an instant, shook his head carelessly, and returned to his measuring, speaking in a loud voice.

His duty finished, he approached me, saying in his loud tones,—

"My good friend, in six months this prison will be greatly improved."

And his gestures seemed to add,—

"You will not enjoy it; what a pity!"

He almost smiled. I thought he was going to tease me, as one might tease a young bride on her wedding-night.

My gendarme, an old soldier with chevrons, replied for me,—

"Monsieur, we do not speak so loud in a death-chamber."

The architect went away.

And I was left there, like one of the stones he had measured.

Chapter XXXII

Then a funny thing happened.

They had taken away my kind old gendarme, whom I had not even shaken by the hand, ungrateful egoist that I am. Another took his place, a man with a low brow, eyes like a cow's, and a stupid face.

I paid no attention to him, but sat before the table with my back to the door. I was trying to cool my brow with my hand, for I was troubled in mind.

A light touch on my shoulder made me turn. It was the new gendarme, who was alone with me.

This is somewhat the way in which he addressed me.

"Criminal, have you a kind heart?"

"No," I replied.

The brusqueness of my answer seemed to disconcert him. But he continued hesitatingly,—

"One is not bad for the pleasure of being so."

"And why not?" I asked. "If you have nothing else to say to me, leave me. What are you aiming at?"

"I beg pardon, my criminal," he replied; "just two words. These: If you could make a poor man happy, without its costing you anything, would you not do so?"

I shrugged my shoulders.

"Do you come from Charenton? You choose a strange vase from which to draw happiness. *I* make any one happy!"

He lowered his voice, and assumed an air of mystery, which was not in keeping with his stupid face.

"Yes, criminal, happy and lucky. You can make me all this. Listen. I am a poor gendarme. My duties are heavy, my pay is small; my horse is my own, and is the ruin of me. But to offset this I take shares in the lottery. One must have some business. Until now I have needed nothing in order to win except lucky numbers. I look everywhere for sure ones; but I always fall to one side. I place 76; it draws 77. In vain have I kept them; they do not come. A little patience, please; I am almost through. But here is a lucky chance for me. It seems—pardon me, criminal— that you are to die to-day. It is a well-known fact that these who die in this way see the lottery in advance. Promise me to come to-morrow evening,—what difference will it make to you?—and give me three numbers, three good ones. Hey? I am not afraid of ghosts, you may be sure. This is my address: Caserne Popincourt, staircase A, number 26, at the end of the corridor. You will recognize me, won't you? Come even this evening, if it is more convenient for you."

I would have scorned answering him—the imbecile!—if a mad hope had not crossed my mind. In such a desperate position one occasionally imagines that a chain can be broken by a thread.

"Listen," I said, acting the comedian as much as is possible when one is about to die, "I will make you richer than the king, so that you can win millions—on one condition."

He opened his stupid eyes.

"What condition? What? Anything to please you, my criminal."

"Instead of three numbers, I promise you four. Change clothes with me."

"If that is all!" he cried, unhooking the top hooks of his uniform.

I rose from my chair. I watched his every movement with a beating heart. Already I saw the doors opening before the gendarme's uniform, and the Place, the street, and the Palais of Justice behind me!

But he turned with an undecided air.

"Ah, is this in order that you may escape?"

Then I knew that all was lost, yet I tried a last resort, which was foolish and useless.

"Yes," I replied, "but your fortune is made."

He interrupted.

"Well, no! Not so fast! You must be dead for my numbers to be lucky ones."

I sat down mute, in greater despair than ever, after the hope I had had.

Chapter XXXIII

I closed my eyes, and raised my hands, trying to forget the present in the past. As I dreamed, thoughts of my childhood and early manhood came back to me one by one, sweet, calm, and smiling, like islands of flowers, across the gulf of black and confused thoughts which were seething in my brain.

I was a child again, a merry, laughing schoolboy, playing, running, and shouting with my brothers in the great green paths of the wild garden where I passed my early years, in an old yard belonging to a convent, over which towered the dark dome of the Val-de-Grâce.

And then four years later, a child still, but dreamy and passionate. There was a young girl in the lonely garden.

Pepa, a little Spanish maid of fourteen, with great eyes, thick hair, a golden-brown skin, and red lips and rosy cheeks.

Our mothers told us to go and run together; but we walked.

They told us to play, but we talked, children of the same age, but of different sex.

There was only one year left for us to run and quarrel together. I argued with Pepita over the most beautiful apple on the tree; I struck her for a bird's nest. She cried: I said, "That served you right!" and we went to our mothers with our complaints; and they told us aloud that we were in the wrong, but whispered aside to us that we were right.

Later she is leaning on my arm, and I am proud and happy. We walk slowly, and speak in low tones. She drops her handkerchief; I pick it up for her. Our trembling hands touch. She tells me about the little birds, about the star which is visible beyond, about the crimson sun setting behind the trees, or about her schoolmates, her dress, and her ribbons. We make innocent remarks, and both of us blush. The little maid has grown into a young woman.

That evening—it was summer—we were under the chestnut-trees, at the end of the garden. After one of those long pauses with which our conversation abounded, she dropped my arm, exclaiming, "Let us run!"

I can see her now; she was in black, in mourning for her grandmother. This childish idea had entered her head; Pepa was Pepita again, as she cried, "Let us run!"

She started ahead of me, her slender waist like a wasp's, and her flying skirts showing her little feet above the ankles, I sped after her. Now and then the wind raised her black tippet, and I saw her soft brown neck.

I was beside myself. At last I caught her near an old ruined well. I seized her by the waist, by right of conquest, and made her sit down on a grassy knoll; she did not resist. She was out of breath, and smiling. I was serious, and I watched her black eyes behind her dark lashes.

"Sit here," she said to me. "It is still daylight; let us read something. Have you a book?"

I had with me the second volume of the *Voyages of Spallanzani*. I opened it at random, and I drew nearer to her; she leaned her shoulder against mine, and we began to read to ourselves. Before turning a page she always had to wait for me. My mind acted less quickly than hers.

"Have you finished?" she would ask when I had scarcely begun.

Our heads touched each other, and our hair; we felt each other's breath little by little, and finally our lips met.

When we turned back to our reading the sky was full of stars.

"O Mamma, Mamma," cried she, as we reached home, "if you only knew how we have run!"

I was silent.

"You say nothing," said my mother. "You look sad." But my heart was a paradise.

That was an evening I shall remember all my life.

All my life!

Chapter XXXIV

Some hour has just struck, but I know not which one; I can scarcely hear the striking of the clock. I feel as though the noise of an organ were in my ears; but these are my last thoughts which make such a hum.

At this supreme moment, when I am lost in these remembrances, I recall my crime with horror; and I want to repent still more. I felt greater remorse before I was condemned; since then it seems as though there was no time for anything but thoughts of death. But I should like to repent.

When I consider for a moment what my life has been, when I think of the axe which is about to end it all, I shiver as though it were a new thing to me. My beautiful childhood! My happy youth! A golden cloth, the end of which is bloody. Between then and now, runs a river of blood; another's blood and mine.

If some day my story should be known, no one, after reading of so many years of innocent happiness, will wish to think of this dreadful year, which began by a crime, and ended in an execution; it will appear odd and out of place.

And yet, oh, wretched laws, and wretched men, I was not wicked!

Oh! to have to die in a few hours, and to think that a year ago, on a day like this, I was free and innocent, taking my autumn stroll, wandering under the trees, and walking among the leaves.

Chapter XXXV

Even at this very moment there are about me, in the homes around the Palais and La Grève, everywhere throughout Paris, men coming and going, talking and laughing; men reading the papers, and thinking of their business; merchants making bargains; young girls planning their ball-gowns for this evening; mothers playing with their children!

Chapter XXXVI

I remember one day when I was a child I went to see the great bell of Notre-Dame.

I was already dizzy from having climbed the dark, winding staircase, and crossed the frail gallery which connects the two towers whence I saw Paris at my feet, when I entered the cage of stone and wood where the bell hangs, with its tongue which weighs an hundredweight.

I advanced tremblingly across the poorly joined planks, looking over at the clock which is so famous among the children and the people of Paris, and realizing, not without some fright, that the slate box about it, with its sloping sides, was on a level with my feet. Every now and then I saw, as the crow flies, so to speak, the Place of Parvis, Notre-Dame, and the people who seemed like ants.

All at once the great bell began to strike; a deep vibration filled the air, making the heavy tower sway. The beams of the floor trembled. The sound almost threw me over. I swayed, and barely escaped falling down the sloping sides of the slate box. In terror I lay down on the beams, grasping them tight with both hands, without speaking, without breathing, with that dreadful noise in my ears, and under my eyes that precipice, that Place far below me, where so many peaceful, enviable people were passing.

Well, it seems as if I were still in that bell-tower. Everything is indistinct and blurred. Something like the noise of a bell shakes the cavities of my brain; and around me I see the calm, tranquil life I have left, which other men are still living; but I see it only from afar, and across the depths of an abyss.

Chapter XXXVII

The Hôtel de Ville is an evil-looking building. It is on a footing with La Grève, with its narrow, pointed roof, its strange belfry, its great white dial, its rows of small columns, its thousand windows, its worn staircases, its two arches on the right and left; sombre and sad it stands, its face wasted away with years, and so dirty that even in the sunlight it is black.

On execution days it emits gendarmes from all its doors, and it watches the condemned man with all its windows.

In the evening, its dial, which marked the fatal hour, still shines out upon its dark façade.

Chapter XXXVIII

It is a quarter-past one.

This is how I feel.

I have a violent pain in my head, my back is cold, my forehead burns. Every time I rise or lean over, it seems as though there were a liquid in my brain which makes it knock against the sides of my head.

I tremble convulsively, and now and then the pen falls from my hand as though by a galvanic action.

My eyes smart as though I were in the midst of smoke.

My elbows ache.

But only two hours and forty-five minutes are left before I shall be well again.

Chapter XXXIX

They say that it is nothing, that one does not suffer, that it is an easy, simple death.

But what is this agony for six weeks, and this rattle for twelve whole hours? What is the anguish of this irreparable day which is passing so slowly and yet so quickly? What is this ladder of torture leading to the scaffold? Is all this "nothing"?

Apparently this is not suffering.

Is it not the same sensation when the blood wastes away drop by drop as when the mind exhausts itself thought by thought?

Then, are they sure that we do not suffer? Who has told them so? Has it ever happened that a bloody head has raised up on the edge of the scaffold, and cried out to the people, "That did not hurt!"

Has any one who was killed in this way returned to thank them, and say, "That is a good invention; do not give it up. The machine is fine."

Did Robespierre? Did Louis XVI?

No! But it is nothing! they say. In less than a minute, in less than a second, it is over. But have they ever put themselves, even in thought, in the place of the one who is there, when the heavy axe falls, tearing the flesh, breaking the nerves, cutting the vertebræ—ah! only half a second! The pain is over—oh, horrors!

Chapter XL

It is strange that I am constantly thinking of the king. In vain have I tried not to, in vain have I shaken my head; there is a voice in my ear which says constantly,—

"In this same city, at this very hour, and not far from here, there is, in another palace, a man who also has guards at every door; a man like you, individual among the people, with this difference,—that he is as high as you are low. His whole life, minute by minute, is but glory, grandeur, delight, intoxication. Everything about him is love, respect, veneration. The loudest voices become low when he is addressed, and the proudest brows humble. Beneath his eyes all is silk and gold. At this very moment he is holding a council of ministers where every one is of his opinion; or he is thinking of to-morrow's hunt, of this evening's ball, sure that the *fête* will come, and leaving to others to plan his pleasures. Well! this man is flesh and blood like you! And in order, at this very instant, for the horrible scaffold to crumble, and all be restored to you,—life, liberty, fortune, family, he need only write with this pen the seven letters of his name, at the bottom of a slip of paper; or it needs but his coach to meet your wagon. And he is good, and would ask for nothing better, perhaps; and yet none of this happens!"

Chapter XLI

Very well, then! Let us be brave with death; let us take hold of this horrible idea with our two hands, and look at it full in the face. Let us ask it what it is; let us know what it demands of us; let us turn it over on every side, and spell out the enigma; let us look at the tomb in advance.

It seems to me that as soon as my eyes shall have closed, I shall see a great illumination, and abysses of light where my spirit shall roll forever. It seems to me that the sky will be lighted by itself, that the stars will be dark spots there, and that, instead of being as they are now to our living eyes, spangles of gold on black velvet, they will seem black points on a gold cloth.

Or, poor wretch that I am, it will perhaps be a hideous and deep whirlpool, the sides of which are lined with shadows, and into which I shall fall forever, seeing other forms moving about in the darkness.

Or, waking after the blow, I shall perhaps find myself on a flat, damp surface, crawling through the darkness, and turning over and over like a rolling head. It seems to me that there will be a great wind which will drive me on, and that I shall be hurled here and there by other rolling heads. At intervals there will be seas and streams of a dry and unknown liquid; everything will be black. When my eyes in their rotation shall turn upwards, they will see only a sky of blackness, the thickness of which will weigh down upon them, and far away at the end will rise great arches of smoke, blacker than the shadows. They will also see, flying in the night, small crimson sparks, which, on coming near, will become birds of fire. And it will be like this through all eternity.

It may be also that at certain times the dead of La Grève will gather together in the black nights of winter on the Place which belongs to them. It will be a pale and bloody crowd, and I shall not be wanting. There will be no moon, and they will speak in low tones. The Hôtel de Ville will be there, with its worm-eaten façade, its fallen roof, and its dial which has been pitiless alike to all. There will be on the Place a guillotine from hell, and the Devil will execute a hangman; this will be at four o'clock in the morning. Then it will be our turn to gather around in crowds.

It is probable that it will be like this. But if these dead return, under what form will they come? What part of their incomplete and mutilated body will they keep? Which will they choose? Will the head or the body be the ghost?

Alas! what does death do with our soul? What nature does it give it? What does it take, and what does it leave with it? Where does it put it? Will it sometimes lend it eyes of flesh with which to look down upon the earth and weep?

Ah! for a priest! A priest who knows all this! I want a priest, and a crucifix to kiss!

My God! it is always the same!

Chapter XLII

I begged them to let me sleep, and I threw myself on the bed.

I had a clot of blood in my head, which made me sleep. It is my last sleep of this kind.

I had a dream.

I dreamed that it was night. It seemed that I was in my office with two or three of my friends, whom I do not remember.

My wife was in the adjoining bedroom, asleep with her child.

We were talking in a low voice, and what we said seemed to frighten us.

Suddenly I heard a noise somewhere in the other rooms of the house. A faint, strange, indistinct noise.

My friends heard it too. We listened; it sounded like a lock opening stealthily, like the noise coming from the sawing of a bolt.

There was something in the air which froze us. We were afraid. We thought perhaps robbers had entered my house at this late hour of the night.

We decided to go and see. I rose and took the candle. My friends followed, one after the other.

We crossed the adjoining bedroom. My wife was sleeping with her child.

We reached the drawing-room. There was nothing there. The portraits hung motionless in their gold frames against the crimson wall. It seemed to me that the door from the drawing-room into the dining-room was not in its usual place.

We entered the dining-room, and walked around it. I went first. The door from the stairway was tightly closed, as well as were the windows. Near the stove I saw that the linen-closet was open, and that the door of this closet was drawn out, as though to hide the wall behind it.

This surprised me. We thought that some one was behind the door.

I raised my hand to close it, but could not. Startled, I pulled harder, when suddenly it yielded, and we saw a little old woman, her hands hanging down and her eyes closed, standing motionless, as though caught in the corner of the wall.

There was something hideous about it all, and my hair stands on end when I think of it.

"What are you doing there?" I asked the old woman.

No answer.

"Who are you?" I asked again.

She neither spoke nor moved, but stood with closed eyes.

My friends said,—

"Probably she is in league with those who have entered with evil intentions; they escaped when they heard us coming. She could not, and hid here."

I questioned her again; but she remained speechless, motionless, sightless.

One of us gave her a push. She fell forward.

She fell like a block of wood, like a dead thing.

We pushed her with our feet, then two of us raised her, and stood her up against the wall again. Still she gave no sign of life. We shouted in her ear, but she was as dumb as though she were deaf.

We were losing patience, and there was anger in our terror. One of the men said to me,—

"Put the candle under her chin." I did so. She half-opened one eye,—an empty socket, dull, frightful-looking, which could not see.

I removed the lighted wick, saying,—

"Ah! at last! Now answer, you old sorcerer! Who are you?"

The eye closed, unresponsive like herself.

"Well, this is too much!" cried the others. "The candle again! The candle! We'll make her speak!"

Again I placed the light under the old woman's chin.

She opened both eyes slowly, looked first at one, then at another of us, and suddenly leaning forward, she blew out the candle with an icy breath. At the same time I felt three sharp teeth clutch my hand in the darkness.

I awoke, trembling, covered with a cold perspiration.

The kind priest was sitting at the foot of my bed, reading prayers.

"Have I slept long?" I asked.

"My son," he said, "you have slept one hour. They have brought your child here. She is waiting for you in the next room. I did not wish them to waken you."

"Oh!" I cried. "My daughter! Tell them to bring her to me, my little girl!"

Chapter XLIII

She is fresh and rosy, and has big eyes; she is beautiful!

They had put on a pretty dress, which was very becoming to her.

I took her, I raised her in my arms; I seated her on my knee; I kissed her hair.

Why had her mother not come with her? "Her mother is ill, and her grandmother too." That is well.

She looked at me in a surprised sort of way. She let herself be petted and fondled, and covered with kisses; but every now and then she threw an anxious look toward her nurse, who was crying in the corner.

At length I spoke.

"Marie!" I cried, "my little Marie!"

I caught her violently to my heart, choking with sobs. She gave a little cry.

"Oh, you hurt me, sir!"

"Sir!" The poor child had not seen me for a year. She had forgotten me,—my face, my words, my voice. Alas! who, indeed, would recognize me with this beard, these clothes, and this pallor? What! already forgotten by the only one whom I wanted to remember me! What! no longer a father, even now! To be condemned never again to hear the word in the language of children, which is so gentle that it cannot belong to that of men,— "*Papa!*"

To hear those lips speak it once more, just once more, this is all I would have asked for the forty years of life that they are taking from me.

"Listen, Marie," I said, taking her two little hands in mine, "do you not know me any more?"

She looked at me with her sweet eyes, and answered,— "No!"

"Look well," I said again. "What! do you not know who I am?"

"Yes," she said; "you are a gentleman."

Alas! to love only one being in all the world, to love her with all one's love, and to have her before you, seeing you and looking at you, speaking to you, and answering you, and not knowing you! To want consolation only from her, the only one who does not know that you need it, and because you are about to die!

"Marie," I asked, "have you a papa?"

"Yes, sir," the child answered.

"Well, where is he?"

She raised her great eyes in astonishment.

"Ah! don't you know? He is dead."

Then she began to cry; I almost let her fall from my knee.

"Dead!" I exclaimed; "Marie, do you know what it is to be dead?"

"Yes, sir," she replied. "He is in the earth and in heaven too."

She went on of her own accord,—

"I pray to the good God for him night and morning, on mamma's knee."

I kissed her forehead.

"Marie, say your prayer for me."

"I cannot say it now, sir. A prayer is not made in the daytime. Come this evening to my house, and I will say it for you."

This was enough. I interrupted her.

"Marie, I am your papa."

"Oh!" she exclaimed.

I added, "Do you want me for your papa?"

The child turned away.

"No; my papa was much more beautiful."

I covered her with tears and kisses. She tried to disengage herself from my arms, crying,—

"Your beard hurts me."

I sat her again on my knees, devouring her with my eyes, and then I questioned her.

"Marie, do you know how to read?"

"Yes," she replied; "I can read very well. Mamma makes me read my letters."

"Well, let us hear you read a little," I said, pointing to a paper, which she was crumpling in one of her baby hands.

She nodded her pretty head.

"Well, I can read only fables."

"Never mind; try. Come, read."

She unfolded the paper, and began to spell out with her finger,—

"A, R, ar, R, Ê, T, rêt, arrêt"—

I snatched it from her hands. It was my death-sentence that she was reading to me. Her nurse had bought the paper for a sou. It cost me more than that.

Words cannot express what I felt. My violence frightened her.
She was almost in tears. All at once she said to me,—

"Give me my paper; it is to play with." I handed her back to
her nurse.

"Take her away," I cried.

And I fell back in my chair, sad, lonely, despairing. They may
come now; I care for nothing more; the last cord of my heart is
broken. I am ready for whatever they want to do with me.

Chapter XLIV

The priest is good, and the jailer also. I think that they dropped
a tear when I said that they might take away my child.

They have done so. Now I must harden myself, and think
with firmness upon the hangman, the wagon, the gendarmes,
the crowd on the bridge, on the wharf, at the windows, and that
which is waiting expressly for me on that gloomy Place de
Grève, which might well be paved with the heads it has seen
fall.

I believe that I still have an hour in which to grow accustomed
to all this.

Chapter XLV

All the populace will laugh, and will clap their hands, and shout.
And among all these men who are free and unknown to the jailers, who run joyfully to an execution, in this crowd of heads
which will cover the Place, there will be more than one which
sooner or later will follow mine into the crimson basket. More
than one who comes there for me will some day come for himself.

For these fatal beings there is, on a certain spot of La Grève,
a fatal place, a centre of attraction, a trap. They turn around
until they finally reach it.

Chapter XLVI

My little Marie! They carried her away to play. She watched the crowd from the cab-window, but thought no more of the *gentleman*.

Perhaps I still have time to write a few pages for her, that some day she may read them, and fifteen years from now, may, perhaps, weep at to-day.

Yes, she must know my story from me, and why the name I leave her is bloody.

Chapter XLVII

My Story

EDITOR'S NOTE.—The pages attached to this cannot be found. Perhaps, as those which follow would indicate, the condemned man did not have the time to write them. It was late when the thought occurred to him.

Chapter XLVIII

A Room in the Hôtel de Ville

THE HÔTEL DE VILLE! So I am here. The wretched journey is over. The Place is not far away; and under the window the horrible crowd is gathering, the crowd which longs and waits and laughs.

I have hardened myself in vain, I have trembled in vain; it is always the same; my heart still fails me. When, above the heads, I saw those two great crimson arms, with the black triangle at one end, standing between the two lanterns on the quay, my heart failed me. I asked to be allowed to make a final declaration. They brought me here, and they have gone for a public prosecutor. I am now waiting for him. It is so much time gained.

Here he is.

Three o'clock struck, and they came to tell me that it was time. I trembled, as though I had been thinking of anything else for five whole hours, for six weeks, six months. It affected me as though it were something unexpected.

They made me cross corridors and descend stairways. They brought me between two jailers to a gloomy, narrow, arched room on the ground-floor, that would be almost dark on a rainy, foggy day. A chair stood in the centre. They told me to be seated. I obeyed.

Near the door and along the walls several men were standing, besides the priest and the gendarmes, and there were three other men also.

The first, the largest and oldest, was fat, with a red face. He wore a cloak and a three-cornered hat. It was *he*, the hangman, the valet of the guillotine. The other two were his valets.

Scarcely was I seated, before the other two came up behind me like cats; then all at once I felt a cold steel run through my hair, and scissors touching my ears.

My hair was cut off, and its locks fell on my shoulders. The man with the three-cornered hat touched them gently with his rough hand.

Around me they were all talking in low tones.

Outside there was a great noise, like a mighty roaring. At first I thought it was the river; but from the laughter which burst out, I knew it was the people.

A young man near the window was writing in a copybook, and asked one of the jailers what they called that which they were doing.

"The toilet of the condemned man," the other replied.

I knew that it would all be described in to-morrow's paper.

Then one of the valets removed my jacket, and the other took my two hands, which were hanging down, and tied them behind me with a rope, which they knotted around my wrists. At the same time the other took off my cravat. My cambric shirt, the only article which remained of my former life, made him hesitate a moment; then he began to cut away the collar.

At this dread precaution, at the touch of the steel on my neck, my elbows shook, and I gave a stifled groan. The hand of the executioner trembled.

"Monsieur," said he, "pardon me! Did I hurt you?"

These hangmen are very gentle.

The shouts of the people outside grew louder.

The fat man with the pimpled face handed me a handkerchief to smell of which was saturated with vinegar.

"Thanks, no," I said, in as strong a voice as I could command; "I do not need it; I am very well."

Then one of the men knelt down, and bound my feet by means of a fine, narrow rope, which allowed me to take only short steps. The rope was attached to that which bound my hands.

The fat man threw my jacket over my back, and tied the sleeves under my chin. All that was to be done there was finished.

The priest approached with his crucifix.

"Come, my son," said he.

The valets took hold of my arms. I rose and walked; but my steps were weak and trembling, as though each leg had two knees.

The outside door was now flung open. The furious shouting, the cold air, and the white light fell on me as I stood in the darkness. At the farther end of the dull prison I saw all at once, through the rain, the thousand howling heads of the populace, crowding pellmell upon the wide steps of the Palais; on the right, on a level with the threshold, was a line of horses belonging to the gendarmes, of which only the front feet and the breasts could be seen from the lower door; in front, a company of soldiers was drawn up in line of battle; on the left, I saw the rear of a wagon, against which a steep ladder was leaning. It was a hideous picture, well-framed in the door of a prison.

It was for that awful moment that I had been gathering all my strength. I took three steps, and stood on the threshold of the prison.

"There he is! There he is!" cried the people. "He is coming out at last!"

And those nearest to me began to clap their hands. If they loved the king very much it would be less of a holiday.

It was an ordinary wagon, with a worn-out horse; and the driver wore a blue smock-frock, with red figures on it like those of the gardeners in the suburbs of Bicêtre.

The fat man with the three-cornered hat was the first to mount.

"Good-morning, Monsieur Sanson!" cried the children on the railings.

A valet followed him.

"Hurray, Mardi!" cried the children again.

Both sat down on the front bench.

It was my turn next. I stepped up with a firm tread.

"He walks well!" said a woman by the side of the gendarmes.

This cruel praise gave me courage. The priest took a seat opposite me. They had put me on the rear seat, with my back to the horse. I shuddered at this last attention.

After all they have some feeling in them.

I looked around me. Gendarmes before, gendarmes behind; then the people, the people, the people; a sea of heads on the Place.

A picket of mounted gendarmes awaited us at the gate of the Palais.

The officer gave the order. The wagon and its procession began to move, as though pushed forward by a howl from the people.

We passed through the entrance; and as the wagon turned toward the Pont au Change, the Place burst out into a cry which echoed from the pavement to the roofs, and the bridges and the quays answered it with the noise of an earthquake.

At this point the picket joined our escort.

"Hats off! Hats off!" cried a thousand voices together, "as for the king!"

I gave a frightful laugh, and exclaimed to the priest,—-"They, their hats; I, my head."

The horses walked.

The quay was sweet with the odor of plants; it was flower-market day, but the women had deserted their posies for me.

Opposite, in front of the square tower which rises at the corner of the Palais, were wine-shops, the doorways of which were filled with spectators, especially women, who were rejoicing over their fine places. The day ought to be a good one for the tavern-keepers.

They were renting tables, chairs, scaffolds, wagons. Everything was crowded with spectators. Merchants of human blood were crying out with all their might,—

"Who wants a place?"

I was filled with rage against all these people, and I longed to shout out,—

"Who wants mine?"

The wagon moved on. At every step the crowd surged up

after it, and it was with fright that I saw more crowds gathering in the distance at other points of my journey.

As we crossed the Pont au Change, I chanced to look back on my right. My eyes fell on the other quay, above the houses, and on a solitary black tower, covered with carved images, on the top of which I saw two stone monsters sitting sidewise. I do not know why I asked the priest the name of the tower, but I did.

"St. Jacques-la-Boucherie," the hangman answered.

I cannot explain how it was; but nothing escaped me in the mist, in spite of the fine white rain which glistened upon everything like the network of a spider's web. Every detail suggested some horror to me. Words fail me to describe my feelings.

Toward the middle of the wide Pont au Change the crowd grew so dense that we could scarcely pass, and I was seized with a violent terror. I thought, final vanity! that I should faint. Then I strove to become deaf and blind and dead to everything except the priest, whose words I could scarcely hear, owing to the shouts of the people.

I took the crucifix and kissed it.

"Pity me, O my God!" I cried; and I tried to lose myself in this thought.

But every jolt of the hard wagon shook me. Then all at once I became violently cold. The rain had soaked my clothes, and dampened my shaved head.

"You are shaking with the cold, my son," said the priest.

"Yes," I replied.

Alas! alas! it was not only from the cold.

At a turn in the bridge, the women expressed pity at my youth.

When we reached the fatal quay, I was beginning to see and hear nothing. The voices, the heads at the windows, at the doors, at the shop-railings, on the arms of the lanterns; the open-eyed and cruel spectators, the people who knew me, and not one of whom I knew; the paved street lined with human faces—I was unconscious of them all; I was dazed and blind. It is a dreadful thing to have the weight of so many eyes bearing down upon one.

I swayed on my bench, paying no more attention even to the priest or the crucifix.

In the tumult about me, I no longer could distinguish the cries of pity from those of joy, the jeers from the sympathy, the voices from the noise; it was all a roar in my head like an echo striking on brass.

I mechanically spelled out the signs on the shops.

Once a strange curiosity made me turn my head to see what was in front of us. It was a last effort of my mind, but the body refused to obey. My neck was paralyzed as though already dead.

I saw on my left, beyond the river, one of the towers of Notre-Dame, which seen from that point hides the other. It was the one on which floated the flag. There were crowds of people there, and they must have had a good view.

The wagon went on and on, the shops passed by, one sign followed another, written, painted, and gilded, and the people shouted and stamped in the mud, and I let myself be carried on as are those in sleep by their dreams.

Suddenly the line of shops ended in a Place; the shouts of the populace became louder, shriller, more joyful than ever; the wagon stopped, and I almost fell forward on the floor. The priest caught me. "Courage!" he whispered. A ladder was placed at the rear of the wagon; he gave me his arm; I descended, took one step, was about to take a second, when—strength failed me. Between the two lanterns on the quay, I had seen a terrible object.

Oh, it was the real thing!

I stood still, swaying back and forth.

"I have a last declaration to make!" I cried in a weak voice, and they brought me here.

I asked to be allowed to write my last wishes. They unbound my hands; but the rope is here, waiting, and the rest is below.

Chapter XLIX

A judge, a commissary, a magistrate of some kind, has just come in. I implored him with clasped hands to obtain my pardon, dragging myself across the floor on my knees. He asked me with a fatal smile if that was all I had to say to him.

"My pardon! my pardon!" I cried, "or, in mercy, five minutes longer!"

"Who knows? Perhaps it will come! It is so horrible to die thus at my age! One often hears of a pardon coming at the last moment. And whose pardon would it be, sir, except mine?"

The accursed hangman! He approached the judge to tell him that the execution had been arranged for a certain time, that the moment was almost at hand, that he was held responsible; and that, besides this, it was raining, and that the machine ran the risk of becoming rusty.

"Oh, in mercy! Wait one moment for my pardon, or I will defend myself; I'll bite!"

The judge and the hangman went away. I am alone. Alone with two gendarmes.

Oh! the horrible crowd with their hyena-like yells!—Who knows if I may not escape, if I may not yet be saved. If my pardon—it is not possible for them not to pardon me!

Ah! the fiends! I seem to hear them coming up the stairs—

Four o'clock

1881

The original manuscript of the "*Last Day of a Condemned Man*" bears these words on the margin of the first page: "Tuesday, October 14, 1828," and at the foot of the last page: "Night, December 25–26, 1828,—three o'clock in the morning."

Note on "The Last Day of a Condemned Man"

1829

We give opposite,[1] for those interested in this sort of literature, the dialect song, with an accompanying explanation, after a copy found among the condemned man's papers, and which is reproduced in this fac-simile in its original spelling and writing. The meaning of the words is given in the handwriting of the condemned man, and in the last couplet there are two inserted verses which seem to be in his writing also; the remainder is in another hand. Probably, struck with the song, but not remembering it perfectly, he tried to secure a copy, and one was given him by some one in the jail.

The only thing which the fac-simile does not reproduce, is the appearance of the paper copy, which is yellow, soiled, and torn.

---

[1] A facsimile of the song's text to which Hugo refers appears on pages 88 and 89. An English translation of the song appears on pages 35 and 36.

C'est dans la rue des mail
ou j'ai été collége' (1)
par trois cognes de rail'(2) don bon fa mi la ré la
Sur mes zigues ont foncé(3) ré la don fa mi la ré

il m'on mit la tortouse(4) ré la don fa mi la ré la
grand maison est aboulé'(5) don bon fa mi la ré
Dans mon trimin(brenconte) ré la don fa mi la ré la
un pugne(f)De Cotin ré don fa mi la ré

voleur tire-a ma longue(8) don bon fa mi la ré la
jue gz fuan en fourraille'(7) offre bon fa mi la ré
ma longue tout en Cobre don bon fa mi la ré la
m'a tu gue a tu donc mozpille'(10) offre don fa mi la ré

(1) empoigne

(2) archers, sbires, gendarmes

(3) ils se sont jetés sur moi

(4) les menottes

(5) le mouchard en armure!

(6) chemin

(7) voleur

(8) ma femme

(9) emprisonne?

(10) qu'as tu donc fait?

J'ai fait faire un Chêne(11) lirlonfa malurette(11) j'ai tué un homme

Son faubourg j'ai enganté(12)lirlonfa malare'

Son faubourg et sa toquante(13)lirlonfamalurette'

et les attaches de fer(14)lirlonfj malurece'

ma langue j'ai part pour versaille lirlonfamalurette

au pieds de sa majesté lirlonfa malure'

elle lui ferra en babillant(15) lirlonfa malurette(15) elle lui présente un flacon

pour me faire? s'pourra elle', lirlonfamalure,

a fo g or journal lirlon fatonalirette'

ma langue j'entafere(16)lirlonfa ma lure'

qu'li fera porté fontange lirlonfa malurette

et des foubours gabuche'(17)larlon famalure

mais grand duc (18) gui s'fait lator la madame

ne par très cuisinier (18) s'toit matame?

s' je de senfe une dame lirlonfamalurette'

ou il n'y a' pns de planche' lirlonfamalure'

(11) j'ai tué un homme

(12) j'ai pris soy argent

(13) se montre

(14) ses boucles de souliers

(15) elle lui présente un flacon

(16) je passerai j'attaqerai

(17) à galochin

(18) le Roi

(19) ma couronne, mon chapeau